ASBURY HIGH

AND THE

MISTAKEN IDENTITIES

Kelly Brady Channick

MAP OF ASBURY

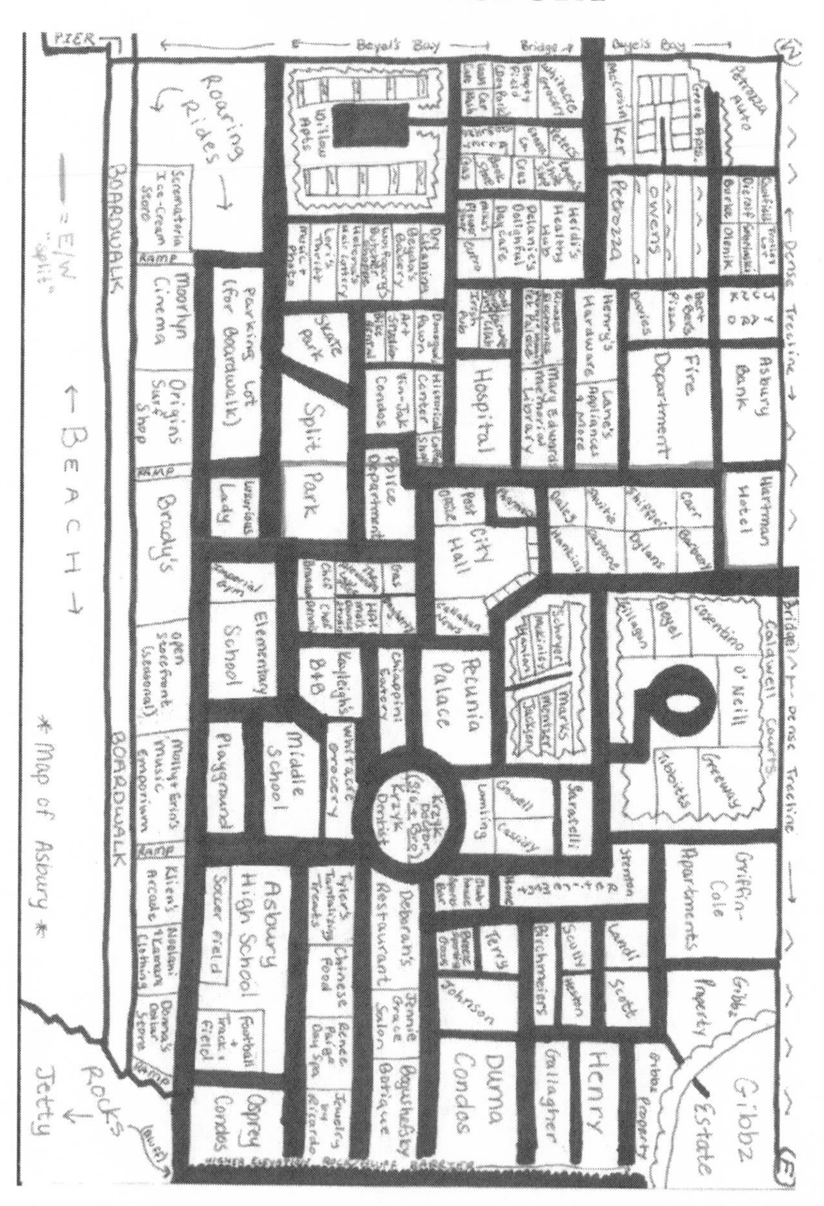

DEDICATION

Ryan, thank you for listening/reading through all of my drafts. You're the best beta reader and an even better husband, I love you.

For more information, email: kbchannick@gmail.com

Cover Designed by: Susan Schafer of Happy Artist Publishers

Created by: Purple Milk Publishing

ISBN: 978-1-7343073-5-1

Other Titles in the Asbury High Series:

Asbury High and the Thief's Gamble

Asbury High and the Parcels of Poison

Acknowledgements:

First and foremost, I would like to thank my incredible husband again. Ryan, your encouragement and never-ending love has turned my dream into a reality. I especially thank you for being the ultimate beta reader and editor-in-chief.

To my amazingly talented cover illustrator, book designer, and trusted advisor, Sue Schafer-Walker. Thank you, you did it again!! I'm so excited for our continuing teamwork.

To my parents and sisters, thank you for the support, humor-filled adventures and creative encouragement.

To all my grandparents: La, Bud, Mary, Edward, Bert, Bev, Marv, and GiGi—you guys started everything, and without you none of this is possible.

To my Aunt Lori, thank you for encouraging my writing, and adding uniqueness to my life.

To my amazing in-laws, Steven and Deborah Channick. Thank you for your support, both through encouragement and last-minute pre-publishing edits.

To my other in-laws: Christy, Alexandra, Steve, Gabriel, Todd and Kurt—for always showing support and making me laugh.

To my two dogs and cat, Dexter, Maui and Donnie. You guys may be crazy, but you're the absolute cure for writer's block.

And once again, my three favorite teachers: **Mr. David Jackson, Ms. Michele Forsman, and Ms. Geralyn Williscroft**. Thank you for encouraging my creativity and happiness. You three were/are the best teachers anyone could ask for!

CONTENTS

1

"What a perfectly bright and sunny day—the perfect day to start off a new school year, with new beginnings, right kids?" whistled the burly, happy postman. And to be honest, any bright day in a coastal town in the beginning of September tends to be rather perfect. The sun is not too hot, and the wind seems to have found its groove. That is, unless there's a hurricane brewing off of the coast. But, luckily for Asbury and its inhabitants, no such storm was in the forecast.

Most people would have just shrugged and walked past Post Officer Samuels, but as a Gibbz, Cornelious was raised to not only converse with adults, but to make them believe he was their equal. Furthermore, Cornelious knew if he didn't form an appropriate response then the mayor, aka his father, would surely hear about it and reproach him for it. In fact, Cornelious could bet that his father would find out immediately, drive up to the Cosentino's in his private limo, and insist Cornelious arrive "in style" (like last year's first day of school) instead of in Mia Cosentino's car. Although Cornelious knew the dangers of driving with the pedal-heavy Mia (who viewed stop signs as optional), he somehow convinced his father that arriving with fellow East Siders would do far more for his reputation. Overall, he was happy with his decision, for at least he'd be making the perilous journey to Asbury High with one of his best friends, Carly.

Even though Cornelious had grown an inch or two over the summer, and now stood at six feet himself, the jolly postman stood at an imposing six foot four, leaving Cornelious looking up in reply. "Yes, sir. It sure is a perfect day to start my sophomore year."

"Sophomore already, Mr. Gibbz?" Postman Samuels scratched his thick, orange beard and pulled some mail from his side satchel. Although the jolly postman had only been Asbury's reliable courier for about two years now, he had made it a point to get to know everyone. It just so happened that on Samuels' first day, Cornelious was at the Petrozza's, since he was there more often than his own home. He and Maddie had opened the door together, not sure what to make of the large, thick-bearded man knocking at her door. Bowing grandly to both thirteen-year-olds, who instantly laughed and took a liking to the man, he explained the importance of introducing himself to every household on the first day of the job. After all, he reasoned, if you can't trust your postman these days, then who can you trust? Cornelious smiled as he remembered Maddie shutting the door after Samuels bounced off her doorstep and replying that at least he wouldn't be reading their mail—like Asbury's last busybody postwoman, Michelle. Even though it was never proven that Michelle had indeed read everyone's mail, the fact that she knew intimate details of most Asburyan's lives, and was forced to constantly wear bandages from all of the papercuts she had received by slitting open the letters, pretty much solidified the accusation.

Bringing Cornelious back to the present, Postman Samuels chuckled and laid a hand on Cornelious' shoulders. "Let me tell you, high school goes by fast. Take my advice… ask the pretty girls out now, before they get away." Samuels winked and handed a pack of letters to Cornelious. Cornelious nodded at the postman and headed up the perfectly manicured walkway to the Cosentino's front door.

As usual, he was impressed that Mr. Cosentino had put himself in charge of landscaping duties, rather than hire someone else to do the job. Not only was that unheard of in East Asbury, but Miles Cosentino proved to be as skilled at yardwork as he was with a camera. Pilot put it best when he said it must be that Miles Cosentino's keen ability to set the stage for the perfect picture translated over flawlessly to the world of landscaping. However, Mr. Cosentino wasn't even aware he had a knack for trimming the bushes or planting beautiful flowers. Carly had confided to the gang that her father had only wanted to teach them the value of hard work. Thus, it was a bonus to discover his hidden talent. Even so, neither Mia nor Carly had ever mowed the lawn nor tended the flower gardens that lined their porch. Still, their parents believed it had set a good example for their children.

Cornelious raised his hand to knock on the giant doors, but was beat to it as Mrs. Cosentino swept him into their foyer beaming brighter than a thousand-watt lightbulb.

"Oh Cornelious! Another year older, and another year even more handsome!" Mrs. Cosentino gushed. She turned to the side to grab a tray from the narrow table which was sitting under the foyer's wide mirror. To Cornelious' stomach's delight, she faced him again, now holding a tray with fresh-from-the-oven, homemade sticky buns she had prepared. Knowing her skill in the kitchen, Cornelious could feel his mouth begin to water.

Thanking her sincerely, he grabbed two sticky buns (seeing as she had made a dozen and neither daughter was likely to eat one, in fear of ruining their first day of school outfit) and smiled.

"It's a new icing recipe from Heidi. It's supposedly loads healthier than regular icing, but you can't tell the difference!" Mrs Cosentino laughed as Cornelious scarfed down both cinnamon buns. Although he had a Western Omelet before leaving his own house, there was no way he could deny the enticing treats set before him. Plus, he argued with himself, he was a growing boy.

As he was reaching for another one, a scream rang out from the floor above.

Mrs. Cosentino sighed, "Oh boy, I'm going to miss these little fights next year."

As a senior, this was Mia's last first day at Asbury High, and she wanted to make sure to leave a good impression. Unfortunately for Carly, the younger sister, that meant Mia would be "borrowing" from her mall-like closet.

Wiping off any remaining crumbs from his lips, Cornelious smiled at the scene unfolding on the staircase. As an only child he had often daydreamed of sibling fights or rivalries—although Maddie had told him that he was crazy and could take one of her five siblings anytime he wanted.

"You are wearing MY earrings though," Carly yelled, clearly deep in an argument with her older sister. Deciding enough was enough, Mia came running down the stairs, keys in hand, with Carly close in tow.

"And you should be thankful. They look great on me." Mia smirked, holding up a hand under each earring, pausing only to check herself over in the large mirror. Locking eyes with him in the mirror, Mia greeted him, "Oh, hi Cornelious. Aren't you looking handsome!"

Cornelious blushed and appraised his own first-day-of-school look. With a new haircut, at his mother's insistence (he had admitted the shaggy hair was getting a bit annoying in a football helmet too), Cornelious Gibbz looked older than a sophomore. His hair was still a dark brown, although lightened a little from the summer sun, but it was shorter than he had ever worn it. Although he wasn't sure what type of haircut he had wanted when he entered Asbury's renown Jennie Grace Salon, where the famous Jennie Grace, herself, was still cutting hair (and yes, the same one who styled celebrities and royalty worldwide), after a quick slideshow of trending haircuts, he had decided to not go "too bold," as Jennie had advised. With a few swift movements from well-skilled hands, Cornelious was left with what Jennie called a "loose undercut." Basically, the sides were much shorter and shaved down, but the top kept most of its thick depth. Overall, he was quite happy with the look and tipped her generously. From the richest kid in Asbury (if not the Western Hemisphere), that meant a lot.

Raking his hand back through his hair, Cornelious smiled at the compliment from Mia, knowing she gave out compliments as often as a celebrity goes without wearing makeup—sparingly, to say the least. In fact, ever since she told Pilot that one of his shirts was cool, he made sure to don it as often as possible around her—to which Carly rolled her eyes and demanded he start wearing other sweatshirts too (to make it clear that he did own more than one outfit).

Turning to face her sister's friend, Mia seemed surprised that she was looking so high up at him now. "Man… you must've grown a few inches while I was on the cruise. I bet you had to buy all new clothes."

Feeling his face growing red, Cornelious admitted his gray jeans and blue shirt were indeed new—but refrained from mentioning how his parents had surprised him just last week with dozens and dozens of new clothes, which were hanging in his dining-room-sized walk-in closet. After all, he wasn't one to talk about his wealth (as he also wished he didn't have as much money as he did).

Mia smirked, "If Trent wasn't so handsome, I'd say you better watch out." Then realizing she had somewhat embarrassed him, she laughingly gave him a quick hug. "I'm kidding! You're like a brother to me… but you seriously are growing up fast. Try not to break too many hearts." Mia winked, as Cornelious found himself feeling more and more uncomfortable. After last year's disastrous crush on Rachel, he found he wasn't really one for dating. And he did have the three greatest friends he could ask for, why would he want to spend time with anyone else?

"You are sooo annoying!" Carly squealed, as she made her way downstairs. Her long, blonde hair swished angrily behind her favorite red hairband, and she stopped halfway to put her hand on her hips. "You're lucky that those earrings would clash with my dress, or else I'd rip them out myself!" Wearing a black and white checkered sunflower dress with red vans, it was hard to imagine Carly Cosentino ripping anything from anyone. But, knowing her actual strength, Cornelious had no doubt in his mind how far she would go.

Apparently, neither did her parents. Exchanging glances, Mr. Cosentino told everyone to freeze, as he whipped out his camera quicker than a Las Vegas wedding ceremony. With a world-renown and government-awarded photographer for a father, Mia and Carly had learned the precious art of dropping everything to take a perfect picture. Cornelious would have laughed, but Mrs. Cosentino thrust him into the picture at the very last moment. The first few frames, Cornelious was sure, probably consisted of him looking dazed or confused. But by the fourth or fifth snap, all three high schoolers could have easily been mistaken for magazine models.

"Oh! These are just perfect!" Mr. Cosentino assessed his work as well as his beaming children.

"Just like the weather," Cornelious mumbled, wondering how often he was going to hear that word today. For him, perfect would have meant more summer and less school.

"You know what else would be perfect? Us getting to school on time," Mia laughed as she glanced at her new, shiny watch. A gift from Trent Petrozza, as their initials were evidently etched on the silver band—clear for all to see.

"And in one piece," Carly grumbled, picturing the perilous road ahead with her sister driving—while praying she wouldn't end up on it.

The three jumped into Mia's baby blue convertible, or death trap, and backed out of the driveway.

"Watch out, Mia! You almost hit Post Officer Samuels' car! That could be a federal crime!" Carly complained, sinking into her seat and mouthing "sorry" to the jolly postman.

"Almost doesn't mean I did," Mia explained, as she straightened out her car and sped towards the grand Asbury High. For most drivers, it would've taken about fifteen minutes to get to the high school from Caldwell Courts, especially on a traffic-heavy first day of school. When Carly opened her eyes to see they had arrived, she wasn't exactly shocked to realize that only seven minutes had flown by.

Unlike last year, with the serendipitous meeting of the gang in front of the grand Asbury High, Mia parked as the last of the students were walking through the giant doors. Though technically not late, Carly and Cornelious rushed inside to find their missing half.

At Asbury High, like many high schools, the lockers you were assigned to your freshman year belonged to you for all four years. Therefore, Carly and Cornelious quickly deposited their bags and headed down the hall to

Maddie and Pilot's lockers. As their last names were close to each other alphabetically, so were their lockers. Maddie and Pilot often bragged that they were likely to always be neighbors, as even their houses justified the idea.

Making their way through the zoo-like atmosphere was anything but easy for the two East Siders. Ignoring teammates or classmates who wanted to catch up in the few minutes before first period, the duo made it to their friends in less than a minute. Even with Carly latching on to Cornelious at one point in order to make through a large crowd surrounding Jason Scott. Cornelious could only imagine what new image he had concocted this year—although his mohawk did seem to do wonders for him last year.

Sensing his girlfriend arriving behind him, Pilot spun around and yelled, "Carly!" Carly jumped into his arms and they shared a quick kiss. Not only as he not into PDA, or Public Displays of Affection, but Principal Coste had implemented strict rules against it. It was rumored that Coste made you kiss each locker door, in the hallway you were seen kissing, as a way to wean you off any further romantic desires.

Maddie's thick, brown ponytail swished around with lightning speed as she turned, juggling notebooks and pencils in her arms. Kicking her locker shut, she smiled at her group of friends and declared, "This school year will be even better than last year!"

Cornelious smiled back and added, "As long as there are no crazy, thieving guidance counselors, it will be…" he paused searching for a word, and decided to use the one that kept popping up today anyway, "perfect."

****

By the time fifth period lunch rolled around, the gang was happy to be sitting together and comparing teachers and classes, with Carly adding the color commentary.

"Apparently Jazz is still dating Johanna, even though she's back in Sweden! Oh, and Nya just broke up with Tone last night! Talk about a rough day of school for him—he was obsessed with her!" Carly's eyes grew wide with excitement. Even if she wasn't one to admit that she enjoyed school, it was the one place where gossip-lovers could get their daily, if not hourly, fill. And, the group agreed her insider knowledge had proven useful on more than one occasion.

Maddie, Pilot, and Cornelious took advantage of Carly's gossip to eat their food, as none of them had anything of value to add. Smiling to himself, Pilot was proud they had managed to have lunch together again—without him having to finagle anything in the scheduling system. Looking across the table at his beautiful girlfriend, Pilot's excitement for the new school year grew. This would be the first school year that he and Carly would be a couple from the start! Looking down at his old, faded jeans and black and white shirt with a simple binary code joke on it (which he wasn't surprised no one understood), he counted himself lucky for his good fortune.

As Pilot and Carly were stuck in their own thoughts, Maddie and Cornelious smiled at each other from over their sandwiches. Once again, the two had every class together, as they made sure to schedule all the same exact classes at the end of each year. Or rather, Cornelious waited for

Maddie to fill out her schedule, copied it, and then they submitted theirs together. But to ensure they had the same periods, Pilot's skills were needed.

"I can't believe we actually have a legit Spanish teacher this year!" Maddie swallowed her food and continued, "I mean last year we had a different sub every other day, and this year we have Senora DiLorenzo, a flamenco dancer from Cuba! And I actually feel like I'm going to be able to learn a lot."

Putting down his peanut butter and jelly sandwich, Cornelious groaned, "I just hope she doesn't only speak Spanish in class."

"That's the best way to learn," Maddie stated, tapping her new black Converses in emphasis.

"And the best way to fail," Cornelious countered.

Maddie laughed and took Cornelious' hand, "You know I'd never let you fail Neal."

Cornelious smiled and once again thanked God he had such a great best friend. Especially now, with Pilot and Carly officially an item and frequently going out on dates, it was nice having Maddie always around.

"Hey, you two are holding hands now? Did I miss that much this summer?" Maddie pulled her hand back, and Cornelious realized she was blushing slightly—which was weird for her, he thought, as he looked up to see his well-groomed, blonde friend Eric Henry, wearing his customary polo and khakis.

"Hey Eric, how was your summer?" Maddie asked.

"Same old, same old. I actually missed it here for once," Eric said, his eyes lingering on Maddie, or at least so it seemed to Cornelious.

"Well, not much happened except for Brady's almost closing down and Asbury's long-lost treasure being found," Carly jumped in, anxious to fill their friend in on what he had missed.

Eric grinned and nodded once. "And I'm sure you four had nothing to do with it."

"Well, we might have aided Asbury's Finest a tiny bit," Pilot conceded, trying to hide a smile.

Eric smiled and explained, "Believe it or not, I heard all about everything from overseas. It's a shame they didn't let you keep any treasure. Jason was bragging about getting a chance to look over the chest. Maria called him, and he told me right after."

"Yeah, would've been nice," Cornelious said, stealing a glance at his friends' stone cold reactions. He reckoned the four of them could compete in his dad's high-stakes poker game, although none of them could probably afford the buy-in (other than himself).

Eric tucked his hands into his pant pockets, and before he could add anything else, was called over to the football table by Jason. Eric knew better than to invite Cornelious over, as those four couldn't even be broken up by Coste himself. Saying goodbye to the gang, he made his way over to the rowdy table a few rows back.

"I still say he likes you, Maddie," Carly sang, biting into her salad and watching Eric turn back to glance over at their table (or most likely Maddie).

Maddie just shook her head, but was grinning nonetheless. Cornelious stared at his friend and wondered to himself if that could possibly be true. After all, they did make-up and become friends again last year…

When the bell rang, the gang was ripped from their little world and continued to their classes. Cornelious and Maddie were happy to make their way to Ceramics, where they had the lovable Miss. D., an Asbury High favorite and their art teacher from last year. Of course, this year, Maddie and Cornelious had a split schedule with Computers and Ceramics swapping every other day, instead of a daily class.

After a quick tutorial of how to use the kiln, where to find the clay, and how to ensure you filled each project with extra love, the class was left to talk amongst themselves and do as they please. Maddie, seeing a handful of soccer teammates in the class, headed over to discuss the double header after school. Much to Maddie's relief (and joy) Senior Captain Dawn had made a quick recovery and would be getting some time today! Coach Pez was still playing it safe and didn't want to start her until she was one hundred percent back to normal. There was no need to risk injury, as the Asbury Aces were vying for a State Title this year.

The period flew by, as did the next. Once again, the gang found themselves all together again, sitting in eighth period Study Hall with Mrs. Cunningham, in the most well-guarded place in the school—the library. For the first day, Mrs. Cunningham had decided to wear an actual dog collar as a necklace, and no one dared reproach her for it. Everyone knew that other than Coste, Cunningham was a staff member not to be messed with. Plus, her strange love of all things animalia was well known, but not quite understood.

Before they knew it, Maddie and Cornelious were

sitting down in their ninth (and last) period class, Honors Chemistry, with the famous Mr. Zam. Not only was he a favorite with students and parents, but was well liked by the faculty as well. Mr. Zam was your average-looking man with close cropped brown hair, big brown eyes, but never went anywhere without his trusty whitecoat. Even in the winter, he would wear his whitecoat over his winter coat. With a unique accent that was fun to replicate, as it was kind of a Southern twang mixed with a robotic voice, students tried their best to engage him in conversation. Conversing with him in a group, however, was often confusing, as he called every student a goon. In fact, he never even bothered to learn most of his pupils' names, and just referred to them as goons.

Luckily, he allowed his goons to pick their own chemistry partners, but warned that unless dire circumstances ensued, they would not be allowed to change. Maddie and Cornelious made their way to the lab table closest to the board. Maddie didn't like to sit in the back and get her view blocked, whereas Cornelious didn't mind either way. The pair was happy that this year, science lab partners were cut down from four to two. Last year, they were stuck with Alexis Johnson and Brittney Anne Saratelli. Cornelious didn't really mind, but he had to hold Maddie back from committing manslaughter multiple times.

"No way, that's not fair. I call being Maddie's partner!" the most annoying voice in all of Asbury boomed from across the room.

"Hey ya, goon! Quiet down!" Mr. Zam declared, making his way around the room with a clipboard for lab partner signups.

"Ed, you can't just claim someone else as yours. There's freedom of choice," Cornelious responded, not knowing if Ed was serous, but knowing Ed and Maddie, or really Ed and anybody, didn't get along.

Ed walked over to where the two were standing and crossed his arms in defiance. "Well, you always get to be with her and get all the answers."

Maddie, choosing to ignore Ed and his nonsense, pulled Cornelious to the front lab table and sat next to him. Ed scowled at the duo but took his seat elsewhere.

"It seems like you've gotten more popular recently," Cornelious muttered, unsure of why he was suddenly so irritated.

Pulling out a notebook and pencil, Maddie laughed. "What can I say? I get better looking each year."

****

At around ten o'clock that night, Maddie climbed into her bed, desperate to enter dreamworld. The first day of her sophomore year had passed without a snag, and she had no complaints. Heck, she even had a hat-trick and two assists in their opener against Lower Township. The boys hadn't been so lucky and had fallen two to one, but she wasn't close with anyone on the team and felt unaffected by their loss. Plus, it wasn't like they lost to Mainland. She shuddered at the thought.

Just as she felt herself slipping into the peaceful darkness behind her eyelids, a soft rapping at the windowpane pulled her back to reality. Pushing the covers aside, she walked across her room to her window and opened it wide for her best friend to enter and join her slumber.

“Thanks. My dad would not stop going on and on about football season and my statistics now that he’s the mayor and all.” Cornelious stepped into the room and pulled out a pair of sweats from his designated bottom dresser drawer. Seeing as Maddie had already crawled back into her comfortable position under her comforter, Cornelious wasted no time in pulling his legs through his sweat pants and slipping on a freshly laundered tee.

Maddie’s eyes were still closed as she fell back into bed, but she saw her best friend perfectly in her mind’s eye. Poor Neal, as she often thought. “I meant to say this earlier, but nice hair cut… Jennie Grace?”

Hearing him chuckle, she opened one eye to squint at him, “Yup. My mom’s idea actually… what do you think?”

Maddie closed her eye and smiled, “You look very handsome, Mr. Gibbz.”

For some reason, Cornelious felt relieved that Maddie didn’t think his new style was dumb or anything. “Anyway, great game today—you killed it!” Cornelious exclaimed as he laid down next to Maddie and recalled each of her goals. “That header off of that corner—woah!”

Maddie grinned as she curled up and fell asleep easily.

Cornelious watched his best bud fall asleep, and not for the first time, envied her room, her family, and admittedly, her life.

2

Most people, parents and children, count down to the first day of school—whether they admit it or not. The date on the calendar is set and nothing short of an act of God can prevent it from occurring. Universally, first day outfits are prepped a few days in advance, with the hope that replications would be rare, and compliments frequent. Therefore, usually the first day of school is easily the most anticipated event in September.

However, due to unforeseen events that had occurred that summer, the first day of school was greatly eclipsed by the second Saturday in September. It was on that second Saturday that a happy crowd formed on the boardwalk, and only continued to swell. Mayor Gibbz not only found his way to the front, but somehow managed to erect a small platform on which he now stood and motioned for the crowd to compose itself. As he delivered a grand, artfully planned speech on the importance of keeping beloved local treasures alive, such as this delicious gem, the crowd listened in an awed silence. Many were already drooling over their soon-to-be-devoured meal.

Although Cornelious had heard snippets of this speech practiced for a few weeks now, he was glad he was on the other side of the glass and didn't have to hear his father take credit for Brady's reopening. Although Jeremiah Gibbz had only been "elected" as the Mayor of Asbury a little over a month ago, when the gang had discovered Ryan Scott's hidden treasure chest, Jeremiah had viewed it as a sign. It was his honest belief that the treasure was awaiting a strong leader to emerge and steer the community in the right direction before it could be found. Cornelious didn't bother pointing out that the treasure didn't just appear, but rather he and his friends had uncovered it after cracking a decades old riddle.

Fortunately for the gang, they had been allowed entrance prior to the opening, or Grand Re-Opening in this case, and were seated in their regular and favorite, corner booth. Brandan and Dennis were furiously working to ensure the place was spotless and the wait staff was primed for the impending stampede of hungry patrons. Although the atmosphere seemed a little tense, a general feeling of relief and excitement flooded the famous eatery. Ready or not world, Brady's was back!

"Denny, hit the lights!" Brandan instructed, standing tall behind the counter with a grin that was so bright, the gang wasn't entirely certain they even needed lights.

"Me pleasure!" Dennis boomed in his best Irish

accent. Taking a deep breath, the six-foot-three, brown-haired, strong chef, flicked the little light switch up with such bravado, you would have thought he was tasked with switching on the nuclear power codes rather than turning on the famous restaurant's renowned sign.

The astronauts peering down at Earth at that exact moment, would've been surprised to witness a giant neon light switch on, and would've quickly been informed that Brady's of Asbury had indeed reopened. And, truthfully, these same cosmonauts were among the first people to place a delivery order to ensure they'd have their delicious dinner awaiting when they returned to the space station.

Back in Asbury, Ms. Owens had already put in the gang's orders, but Dennis and Brandan needed no instructions to their "heroes" as they had rightfully deemed the foursome. Even in the busy rush of customers, the two chefs made sure to personally serve the gang's breakfast and thank them, yet again.

"That was even better than I remember." Pilot sighed, leaning back and pat his full stomach.

"My dreams didn't even do it justice." Cornelious agreed. Pushing his empty plate forward, he considered whether or not he could handle another helping.

"You got that right!" The gang turned their heads to see their favorite twins leaning against the counter. Although they looked alike physically, their hobbies and dress made many forget they were even related.

"Hey Peetie! Long time, no see." Maddie smiled up at her well-dressed, scholarly friend, and most likely future President of the United States.

"Tell me about it. I had Model UN all summer.

Made some cool friends and… interesting contacts." In her typical blazer, and pencil skirt the gang had no problem picturing her at Model UN solving world issues. What was hard to conceive was that the shirtless boy wearing a guitar and fringed jean shorts standing right next to her was her twin brother.

Jazz put his arm around his sister. "I know she was saving the world, but I sure did miss her." The two smiled at each other, and Maddie couldn't imagine ever publicly (or even privately) admitting to missing one of her siblings. She supposed she would, but she saw enough of them as it was.

"I admit, when I heard someone had actually agreed to date this guy," Peetie smiled, and hooked a thumb towards her brother, "I thought they must have some serious brain damage," she joked.

Jazz acted as if he had been stabbed in the heart, "Ouch, man." Everyone laughed, and Jazz surprisingly turned to Cornelious and Carly. "So… uh, I know Peetie's been saying it for years, but Johanna and I have had some pretty deep talks." All four teens kept their faces blank, but couldn't imagine the Swedish bombshell having any depth. They all realized they had been judging her all summer—or in the boys' case, ogling her—but never took the time to actually talk to her, other than racing for her help in times of need. Jazz, looking a little awkward, continued, "Anyway, she convinced me that the anger I've always had against half of the town isn't really justified, and… well… I'm sorry if I was ever rude." Holding out his hand, Cornelious gladly shook it, confirming all was fine. Peetie smiled at her brother's sudden maturity, and the twins turned back to grab their incoming order.

After the twins were served their breakfast and found a seat across the room, a glass was shrilly rung a few times, and a shush rendered the room silent. All heads turned to the front counter where an elderly, smartly-dressed woman in a tight bun and long black skirt proudly stood.

"As you all know, this summer was monumental in our town's history. I dare say the actions of a few saved the precious history of Asbury." Mrs. Geralyn Croft slightly cocked her head to the group and winked. "Today is a day of celebration, as we are blessed to have our favorite taco-pancakes back on our plates." Geralyn paused as those in attendance cheered and clapped. Waiting until they were finished, she resumed. "Brandan and Dennis have given their all to this town for years, and we are forever grateful. For we all know a restaurant is more than just a place to eat, but it is a place to gather, which is exceedingly important for us humans in this day and age," Geralyn chuckled.

Cornelious thought about what she had said and agreed. He and his friends had way too many memories and breakthroughs at Brady's. What would've happened if they never reopened? He shuddered at the thought.

"I won't go on much longer—no one likes a long-winded geezer." Some laughter broke in at this. "But I will remind, or inform, those here that Brady's chefs decided to reopen today, for they knew the importance of such a day. For those who do not remember or even realize, today is Asbury's Ancestors Day, and what better way to pay homage than to gather around and reminisce. You may even learn something important." Geralyn smiled and did a slight curtsy as she took her seat to general applause.

"Just think, she probably would've left town if that historical center didn't randomly get that huge, anonymous contribution a few weeks ago," Carly pointed out, her gaze lingering on Cornelious.

He blushed and took another bite of the new taco-pancake that Ms. Owens had magically placed in front of him. "I don't know. She loves Asbury with all her soul. I don't think she could've left."

Carly shrugged and Maddie smiled. "Either way, I'm glad everything worked out. Like she said, who knows what information we could've lost."

Carly sighed. "You probably think we're going to need it to solve some case in the future."

Pilot, Cornelious, and Maddie smiled in return. Other than Principal Coste's consistent anger and frustration at life, the only other thing they could bet on was that they'd be involved in another case. Mysteries were drawn to the fearless foursome, like flies to a UV-A light—once set on course, there was no avoiding it.

"In the very least, her knowledge might come in handy for a killer college essay topic," Maddie stated, scooping the last bite of her cookie salad into her mouth.

"College? Already, Mads?" Cornelious couldn't even imagine what might happen in three days, let alone three years.

"It never hurts to be prepared."

Pilot was going to explain why getting into college wasn't going to be a problem for any of the four friends—due to his technological skills—when a group of four colorful, older women, probably in their nineties (if not older), squeezed their way to the counter and propped themselves up on four stools. It seemed to Pilot that the older ladies got, the smaller they also became. Yet, he couldn't imagine his own mother or Carly or Maddie growing so small, so he figured it must just be a generational thing. Either way, the four older ladies not only took up space, but they hijacked any conversation around them, due to their partial deafness.

"That's what I said!" yelled the one in a long, red jacket with long, white hair. "I want ONE PANCAKE."

"Anyway, Jodie," continued another lady in a completely yellow outfit, "Our ancestors would've loved this place, but today they would've been too busy."

"Ahh yes!" boomed the largest of the women. She was still very short but was so round that she gave the impression of a walking globe. "Today would have been jury verdict day!"

For once, Carly's rumor-radar wasn't the only one's going off. The gang listened in, hoping to hear some juicy gossip. Not that they needed to be sneaky about eavesdropping, for the four old friends were basically yelling their conversation at each other.

"I still say, McKinley was innocent! There was no hard evidence back in 1828," the frailest looking one dressed in all purple proclaimed. "And the poor man had to face the jury of five of the seven Pecunia founding families, in Pecunia Palace of all places! He was guilty the second he walked in!"

Maddie was thinking this topic would be interesting to investigate, while Carly was praying they wouldn't be dragged into anything close to two hundred years old! Pilot and Cornelious were also listening but were deep into another round of breakfast (at this rate, soon to become lunch).

“Woah, slow down Gibbz, my man! Are you trying to be a lineman this year?” Jason Scott clapped his hand on his friend’s back and smirked at the foursome. His mohawk was freshly back in action, and he had grown more muscular over the summer—causing Pilot to groan inward, as he knew how fond Jason was of his girlfriend.

“Just hungry for victory,” Cornelious replied, smiling at his fellow teammate, but not really wanting to converse with him while he was with his gang. For the most part, Jason was easy to be around. But for some reason, as soon as he got around Pilot and Maddie, he acted superior and the atmosphere was quick to change from relaxed to tense.

“That was pretty corny,” Eric said, stepping back from the counter with an over-flowing tray in his hands. “Hey guys, did you hear the Mainland footballers have been bragging they’re going to whoop us this year?” Although he asked all four teens sitting in the booth, Carly smiled as she noticed how Eric was only looking at Maddie as he asked.

“Seriously?” Cornelious questioned incredulous, thinking about how there was no way that would happen. Maybe if Mainland played as well as they talked trash, they’d have a chance. Cornelious knew that wouldn’t happen, for Mainland and hard work was as opposite as night and day. Perhaps even more opposite, if possible, seeing as night and day worked together in a sense.

"Yeah," Eric continued, eyes twinkling, "We don't play them for another few weeks, but they're already out for blood."

"Now, even I can't wait for the bloodbath," Maddie assured him. If there was one thing Maddie enjoyed more than mysteries, it was crushing Mainland.

Jason grinned. "It sure will be a bloodbath. Mainland always cheats and now they've got a new quarterback."

"Why is twenty-three cents so important in football?" a dreamy voice asked as two girls made their way over to the increasingly crowded corner booth.

"Oh Hannah. A quarter is worth twenty-five cents, remember? And a quarterback is the name of the person who throws the football," Alexis Johnson patiently explained, as if to a newborn, while tossing her perfectly curly, red-hair over her shoulder. She made sure to sidle right up against Cornelious' shoulder, while also staring at Maddie. Maddie ignored her and said hi to Hannah.

Jason smiled and appraised the two girls who had joined them. "I must say a summer away has made you two even more beautiful."

"Oh, you're such a suck-up." Alexis giggled, "But thanks. I admit being on TV has changed my outlook on life."

Thankfully, her sidekick didn't get the hint that Alexis was trying to brag. "I haven't eaten here since it closed," Hannah stated, straightening her blonde bob and looking around at all the happy customers.

"Yeah, no one has," Carly replied, "seeing as it was closed."

The group laughed, including Hannah, although she was unsure what was so funny. Although, admittedly, that tended to happen to her a lot.

"You girls want to eat outside with Henry and I," Jason asked, motioning to his and Eric's gigantic tray of food.

"Sure," Alexis readily agreed.

Clearly not wanting to sit with the two cheerleaders, Eric's face fell. Not noticing, nor caring, Jason ushered his friend towards the boardwalk exit. The four hungry teenagers had just reached the doorway when Alexis turned back and was at the gang's booth once more. "I just wanted to apologize Maddie, and I'd like to be friends."

The gang froze. Although no one could ever be sure about much, the gang was certain that Alexis Johnson and Maddie Petrozza were as destined to be friends as were a killer whale and an already helpless and bloody baby seal.

Maddie felt all eyes on her and exhaled, "Okayyyy… what do you mean?"

Alexis let out a deep breath and looked down. "I feel like I've been unfair to you and rude for no reason. We have a lot in common… actually… and even have most of the same friends. Maybe we could, uh, bury the hatchet and move forward."

Maddie looked into Alexis' innocent, wide eyes and felt that if there was a hatchet involved, one of them would have already used it against the other long ago. However, she decided it was safest to play along. "Okay, I agree. Um, see you in school Monday?"

Alexis' smile shone brighter than the neon Brady's sign glowing outside. "Perf! See ya Monday!"

The gang waited until Alexis had safely left the building before rounding on Maddie.

"What was that about?"

"What's going on?"

"Something is up."

Maddie listened to her friends' concerns and took a big bite of her cookie salad. Swallowing, she looked at Alexis sitting in the distance. "I agree. Something is going on and she doesn't want me in the way… I'll have to be on my A-Game."

"Which means we all do, too," Pilot pointed out.

3

About a month later, it was mid-October and school had been underway for a little over a month. The Senior class, fresh off their senior summer cruise, felt nostalgia for their peaceful time at sea. Maddie had bet Cornelious that her brother and Mia would return broken up, for she never truly viewed Trent as romantic. Cornelious happily took the bet, since being Trent's teammate in football provided him with another view of his best friend's brother.

As guys were apt to do, whenever conversations sprung up over school hotties, Trent never allowed any teammate to mention Mia, whether inappropriately or not, and Cornelious even watched as he kissed a picture of the two of them before leaving the locker room prior to the start of each game or practice. Needless to say, Maddie lost the bet and on the first day of school had to wear a strange bright pink t-shirt picturing an Asian barbie-doll, that they had found earlier in the summer at Lori's thrift. Believe it or not, she had received some compliments and Milton Davies had asked if she was a fan of the show (apparently his younger sister Kimi, one of Shannon and Daniel's close friends, was a huge fan).

Though the weather had gotten colder and the days had grown shorter, the homework and course load pile had only grown larger. It seemed to the students that wearing heavier jackets had provided the teachers with a reason to give them heavier homework. The students didn't complain too much, for a fall without a hurricane in a coastal town makes any weather bearable.

For sophomores this was their first year they were allowed to enroll in AP classes, which Maddie excitedly signed up for, and Cornelious dutifully followed suite. Cornelious knew he was extremely lucky to have Maddie Petrozza as his best friend. Not only had she given him a good luck snack bag filled with all his favorites (Oreos, a smores pop tart and a KitKat bar), but she had helped him retain his focus throughout the day. Usually, Cornelious prided himself on his focus. Or moreover, his ability to prioritize the day's events.

As a student, he received good grades and never really found school to be too difficult. Yes, some classes and tests were harder than others, but he'd just study and do his best. Luckily for him, his best usually resulted in a B or even an A.

As an athlete, he succeeded in every endeavor through sheer force of will and hard work. When he couldn't sink a three pointer, he'd spend hours with Maddie in the park. If he was feeling slow, he would force himself to do timed trials on the track. Even Jeremiah often proudly remarked on his son's drive—and amazingly took no credit.

Therefore, it was clear Cornelious knew how to succeed and plan. However, with Jason and the upperclassmen continuing to gossip about Mainland's amazing new quarterback, Cornelious was feeling anxious. Multiple times throughout the day, he zoned out only to get a sharp nudge from Maddie bringing him back to reality. He shuddered to think what would have happened if they didn't sit next to each other in every class.

By six o'clock, Cornelious was more ready than ever to takedown his rivals. This year, they were playing on Mainland's turf. And most likely, Mustang-friendly refs were employed. As Cornelious went through the motions of warming up, he looked to the stands and easily spotted his friends. Carly was on top of some cheerleader pyramid, already yelling and smiling. And Maddie and Pilot were huddled together on the bleachers, wrapped up in a red and black blanket and some conversation.

"You ready, man?" Jason Scott asked, jogging over to stretch next to him. Whether superstition, or his own version of intimidation, Jason refused to put his helmet on until the last possible moment. Cornelious figured it was another strategy taught to him by his famous NFL playing father, TJ.

Jumping up from his stretching position on the ground, Cornelious fist bumped his friend. "Let's tame those 'Stangs."

*****

"Well fine folks, it's a hearty halftime here at

Mainland Regional High School and our Mighty Mustangs are only up by a fantastically gallant field goal! Show your spirited support for our tireless team and stop on by the scrumptious Snack Bar!" boomed an excited voice over the loudspeaker outside the game box.

Maddie tsked, "That guy sure loves his alliteration."

"I don't exactly want to show my support, but I sure am cold," Pilot murmured to Maddie, as the two were snuggled close together under Ms. Owen's homemade Asbury Aces blanket. Maddie always told Jenna she ought to sell her homemade items for profit, but she had only chuckled, skeptical of her own talent.

Blowing warmth into her frozen, cupped hands, Maddie agreed. "I know what you mean… plus, getting hot chocolate isn't exactly supporting them."

Seeing as it was eight thirty and not getting any warmer or brighter out, the two friends decided to head to the scrumptious Snack Bar and sip on some much-needed hot cocoa. It seemed that the whole population of both Mainland and Asbury had come out to support their boys in their battle. By the time Pilot and Maddie had maneuvered and pushed their way through the crowd and to the front of the Snack Bar, there was only ten minutes left in the thirty-minute Halftime.

"We'll have two hot chocolates please," Maddie ordered, moving her purple Billabong satchel to the front.

"Make that three, ma'am," a loud laugh rang out from behind the duo. Before Maddie could correct the order, the lady had poured three cups of hot chocolate and angrily handed them out the window. Pilot noticed that the Snack Bar attendants were less than friendly to those wearing the red and white Asbury colors.

Maddie scowled at the large blonde boy in the leather bomber jacket. Staring up at the boy she had known since moving to Asbury, she couldn't fathom that it was possible for him to still be growing. Yet, here he was, well over the six foot two inches he was measured at last year, and with a good amount of girth to fool others into mistaking his meanness for strength.

"I won't tell your boyfriend out there," JB motioned to the football field, "that you're buying me gifts now. Unless you want to make this a regular thing." The Pitbulls laughed at their leader, as if he was a grand comedian.

Maddie paid the lady at the window and stepped toward JB and the few Pitbulls gang members he had brought with him. "You owe me a dollar."

JB's grin disappeared, "I'd say you owe me quite a few things… I'll accept this generous gift of hot cocoa though… as a start." With his free hand, JB snapped his fingers. The Pitbulls took this gesture as their cue to step in front of JB, then turn as one and walk back to the bleachers.

"I can't believe JB is smart enough to have that many followers. I swear there are more kids each time we see them," Maddie sipped her hot drink and the two began walking back to their seats.

Try as they might, squeezing their way back onto the stands proved impossible. Not wanting to miss any action, they jammed into a small hole in the crowd leaning against the gates surrounding the track and football field.

"This is actually a pretty good view," Pilot tried to be positive, although he couldn't see Carly cheering from this angle.

Grateful for their Asbury High pride blanket, the two huddled together behind the endzone and were forced to rely on the announcer's ability to describe the game. In this case, the announcer was a pure-bred Mainlander whose commentary was bias, to say the least.

Maddie exhaled, her breath visible in the cold, dark night. "At least we have a full view of the scoreboard."

Both teams took the field and Maddie was surprised to see Cornelious running out on special teams. She always liked coaches who changed things up and had a good feeling about whatever was about to happen. As usual with her gut instinct, she was right on par. Mainland punted the ball to start and the home fans cheered as the ball flew down the field looking like it was going to fall behind the five-yard line. The cheers abruptly stopped when a quick-flying Cornelious Gibbz caught the ball perfectly and sprinted up the field. Either Mainland wasn't ready or didn't have the ability to stop him, for Cornelious returned the punt all the way down the field for a touchdown. Once again, Coach Cap exhibited his quick thinking and creativity in play calls—not to mention his exceptionally thunderous voice was clear to all over the rambunctious crowd, as Cornelious reached the endzone.

As the away team went wild, the atmosphere changed and there was no turning back. Asbury High put the pedal to the metal and scored three straight, virtually uncontested, touchdowns. Halfway through the fourth, many fans began to trickle out and head home. It was no longer a game, but a slaughter.

Maddie and Pilot kept their places at the gate and quickly realized they were next to Mainlanders. Since they were already trouncing them bad enough, Maddie didn't feel the need to engage with any Mainlnaders, and wondered if she should pity them—but the remembered who they were, and instead laughed quietly to herself.

"All I'm saying is, it's a good old-fashioned case of identity theft. It happens online every day and a lot of people keep the same password for every website they use or bill they pay," a tall brown-haired boy leaned on the gate, and shrugged. "Identity thieves have never had it easier."

"Let's say you are right, John. But if it's identity theft, how come my dad—the Sheriff—hasn't found any traces of online sabotage?" A leaner, black-haired kid questioned.

"I don't know. Maybe they're smarter than your dad. Maybe they created their own software or something and are computer-geniuses! I'm telling you though, it's identity theft."

Leaning further over the fence, as if to stress his point, the Sheriff's son continued, "Yeah, well my dad thinks it's just a matter of a few people spending more than they have and not realizing they over-drafted their accounts."

"That's because it doesn't take much to be the Sheriff of Mainland," Pilot whispered. Or so he thought he whispered, until he noticed Maddie cringe and heard his voice carry louder than he intended.

The two boys leaning on the gate next to them, snapped their heads to Pilot. Perhaps looking at the score and feeling the need to stand up for their town, or maybe strangely feeling emboldened after witnessing the lack of effort put forth by their team, it was evident the two teenagers weren't going to let Pilot's comments go.

"And what is that supposed to mean?" the tall boy named John asked, stepping up to face Pilot.

Knowing Pilot's shortage of strength in times like this, Maddie pushed herself in between the two, "The fact that you don't know what it means, explains it all." She honestly hadn't meant to start any trouble or make the situation worse, but sometimes Mainlanders got under her skin and there was no turning back.

A few other Mainland students had sensed trouble and seeing as the game wasn't worth watching anymore, made their way over to where Maddie and Pilot were standing off against their own two high-schoolers.

Glancing around at the slowly-building group of onlookers, it seemed cooler heads prevailed. "I think we just have a disagreement here," the Sheriff's son stated. He took a step forward and pulled his enraged friend back. Just as Maddie and Pilot thought they were in the clear, the Sheriff's son turned back and spit right on Pilot's face.

No one had time to react before JB and the Pitbulls came flying in and tackled the two Mainlanders to the ground. As self-declared defenders of the West Side, Maddie supposed she should've expected the bullies to jump at the chance to defend their hometown. Or more likely, use it as an excuse to get into a highly desired physical altercation. While more and more Mainlanders and Pitbulls threw themselves into the mix, a full-out brawl began, leading to more tackling here than in the game.

Cornelious, standing on the sidelines as the JV squad was put into the game for the final minutes, groaned and prayed the fight going on beyond the endzone had nothing to do with his friends. He squinted over and was relieved to see Maddie and Pilot making their way across the bleachers, and nowhere near the fight. Relieved that for once Maddie had avoided a fight, he turned to talk to his squad when he caught sight of Carly angrily standing with her pom poms on her hips and shaking her head at Pilot. Sighing, Cornelious realized he should've known better.

4

Although Pilot and Maddie could now boast, albeit secretly, about their substantial savings, they knew if they didn't work at the annual Gibbz' Halloween party people might be suspicious. It was almost as much of a tradition for the two of them to be working the party, as it was for the party to be thrown. In the very least their parents would ask where their money was coming from—and unlike the Cosentinos, Maddie and Pilot weren't so sure her parents would let them keep their treasure. Plus, the two teenagers weren't entirely certain they wanted to be guests at the party—where they'd be expected to mingle and have bouts of small talk with other guests, instead of pigging out on the loads of spare candy in the corners, as they were apt to do towards the end of the bash each year.

So, the two friends found themselves stacking up their serving trays and adjusting their pirate costumes in the kitchen of Asbury's grand Pecunia Palace. The kitchen was the only room in the Palace that did not get decorated for any event. Whether it was to save money on the decorations, or whether Head Chef Ski did not wish to have her place of work (and Ski's place worship), devalued, no one could say. Not even Jeremiah Gibbz was willing to take on the scrawny, blonde-haired but steel-backboned Chef from New York. Though she had lived here the better part of twenty years, her Bronx accent was as strong as ever, and her will was enforced by those around her. Which was why catered events at Pecunia Palace were always flawless.

"Kind of ironic we have to dress as pirates when we already found the treasure," Pilot smirked, stroking his fake goatee and adjusting his belt.

Ignoring her friend, Maddie checked the mirror hanging on the wall and fixed her eye patch. Grumbling she asked, "Why did I get stuck with the eye-patch AND the stupid stuffed bird?"

Pilot laughed knowing that Jeremiah Gibbz liked to find novel ways to make his son's friends uncomfortable, to say the least. And given the tense relationship between Mr. Gibbz and Maddie, Pilot wasn't surprised that Maddie had been assigned the worst of the costumes. He was only surprised that she wasn't forced to stand on the plank that hung off the main hall's balcony. "It's a part of the girl costume," Pilot offered.

Before the two could further discuss their costumes, and the fact that no other girl servers had an eye patch nor a parrot attached to their shoulders, Mrs. Nancy Gibbz burst through the doors and announced to the staff it was time to 'man ship' and take their positions out on deck. Clearly, she was very into this year's theme, as she was able to dress cutely and not drearily—which was her opinion of last year's Creatures of The Night theme.

It was nearly seven o'clock and the workers found their ways out into the main hall. Once again, the Gibbz had transformed the Palace into a work of art. Magnificent art was crafted onto each window, making it appear as if stormy seas abounded just outside. Gold pieces and doubloons were strewn across the floor and tabletops. The punch on every table, was labeled as rum—although the guests were assured alcohol was only served at the bar. A wobbly plank was securely nailed to the end of the high balcony, overlooking the hall. Even the floors had been either replaced or covered, no one could be sure, with ship-like wood.

Of course, the real health-inspectors—not the red woman from the summer who was currently awaiting trial—were paid off, and the evening seemed to be yet another success. Pretty much every high-profile East Sider was accounted for and in high spirits. It was Governor Gibbz's first Halloween Bash donning the hat of Mayor Gibbz as well, and he needed it to be picture-perfect. Like everything else in his life.

Being charged with the tray of hor d' ourves, Maddie was making her rounds. Guests seemed squeamish at the little cups full of greenish-brown coagulated gruel, but after assurances from Maddie it was quite delicious (all servers had to taste test what they served, leaving Maddie to semi-joke that Jeremiah could innocently poison them this way), the guests hungrily slopped down their food.

Maddie had to admit it was rather delicious, as she snuck herself a few hor d' ourves throughout the night.

"And what is in this… gruel?" Postman Samuels questioned, as he held the clear cup up to the light and it's wiggled the greenish-brown content.

Maddie explained that they weren't told the ingredients but assured him it was, 'quite delicious'. After gulping down one cup, he smiled and grabbed another. Maddie glanced around and saw that although the guests were predominantly residents of East Asbury, Jeremiah had done his best to ensure all civil servants were invited. Hoping to see Officer Chip dancing around in some swashbuckling attire, she peered around the burly postman, but to no avail. Apparently, justice never rests—although Carly pointed out later that both Officers Swanson and Tennett were busy slurping down the rum all night, and not the fake-kind centered on each table.

Looking over Postman Samuels' choice of costume, Maddie had to ask, "Umm, Mr. Samuels. Can I ask why you wore your work uniform to a costume party?"

Postman Samuels, clad in his cleanest standard-issued Post Officer apparel, including his (empty) mail sash, smiled. "It's the best costume I own." With that statement he winked and rejoined the general public. Maddie watched as the friendly postman clapped various townspeople on the back and was easily accepted by all. Apparently, Asbury's mistrust of those working for the Post Office was long forgotten.

The lights dimmed and swashbuckling music began to play. Maddie made eye contact with Pilot and Carly (who had found each other immediately upon Carly's entrance dressed like Kiera Knightley from Pirates of the Caribbean), looked across the room at each other and grinned. It was time for the Gibbz' grand entrance. Not even the crickets brought in from Africa (to enhance the buccaneer-realism), dared chirp.

"ARRRRRRR you ready for some fun on this treasured Halloween night?" Jeremiah Gibbz boomed from the top of the stairs. As he gallantly stepped into view on top of the grand staircase, his wife—ever the beauty queen—stoically joined his side and thrust her sword (Maddie hoped it was fake, Cornelious knew it wasn't) high into the air. Standing at six foot five inches and participating in a rigorous daily workout regimen, left Jeremiah Gibbz with an impressive stature. Tonight, he seemed even taller and broader, in a classic white, ruffled pirate shirt that was unbuttoned halfway revealing a strong chest (leaving many to swoon and his only son to gag). Adding to this picture of strength was his gorgeous wife, with her long black hair running wild and loose down her sides, in a tattered knee-length pale dress. Even Cornelious admitted that the wild look his mother employed for tonight had made her even more beautiful than usual.

As the handsome couple smiled and waved to those below, the scene changed abruptly. Out of nowhere the lights flickered and a sound of thunder boomed across the Palace. Two rival pirates swung down from the rafters and dropped in front of Jeremiah and Nancy. Without hesitating, the Gibbz' nodded to each other, and a brief, but victorious battle ensued.

When the two invaders had succumbed to their deaths, Cornelious stepped out from behind his parents and sheepishly held a treasure chest out in front of him. The Asburyans clapped and went wild for the show.

Cornelious was glad the chest concealed his face. With his current hairdo much shorter than usual, Jeremiah arranged for a professional make-up artist come in and give his son professional pirate-dreads, which greatly resembled Captain Jack Sparrow. Though he also wore knee-high black boots, and a tattered blue jacket, he drew the line at mascara, for which his parents were adamant. Luckily, the make-up artist was slightly behind schedule and arrived in Asbury two hours later than promised. Therefore, Cornelious was overjoyed to forgo any makeup. When he told his friends of his good luck in that regard, Carly had offered to help, but Cornelious quickly hushed her—hoping his mother wouldn't overhear and accept her offer.

To be honest, this was the second most embarrassing Halloween Ball entrance yet. Second only to the Lion King entrance, where he was Simba, back in the fifth grade. Yes, he was hoisted high in the air above the town and his peers. And yes, he was in a full lion cub suit, with his mother as Rafiki, who made sure to smear a neon orange sticky paste across his forehead. Carly claimed the smell lingered for a whole month, and no one argued with her. Luckily, no one thought to film the scene, and no video existed of his greatest embarrassment.

As the hosts made their way down the stairs and into the main hall to join their guests, it seemed everyone was vying for their attention. Cornelious made eye contact with his friends but knew that would most likely be it for the night. Or at least for the party, Cornelious reminded himself, as he knew he would be crashing in Maddie's room after this. Laughing and snacking on all of the leftover candy, while recalling the craziest costumes, and moments of the night.

As a Gibbz, Cornelious knew all his fellow Asbury citizens, at least by name. When Nancy Gibbz had informed Cornelious that they would be moving to the beach, after he had finished kindergarten, he was afraid he would never make friends. Rather sweetly, she looked up some business owners, and residents of importance, and made flashcards for him to study all summer. Of course, when Jeremiah discovered his son's knack for memorization and recall, he was quite impressed. He also instructed Nancy to add ten more people each week. Thus, seven-year-old Cornelious Gibbz knew almost every citizen of Asbury before stepping foot in the town. Of course, the only three he cared about were the ones he met on the playground after he knocked out a big bully, on the first day of school.

After an hour or so of greeting the more prominent guests--Cornelious was surprised to see a peculiar pairing. In fact, it took him a second and a complete triple-take, to realize that the beautiful woman dressed up in rags with a red, battered overcoat hanging from her shoulders was none other than Ms. Owens! He was equally stunned to find that she had not come alone, and for the first time in his life, Cornelious saw she was with a man.

And not just any man. The tall, dark, and handsome pirate standing next her in a matching red, beaten-up overcoat was his current AP US History I teacher, Mr. Chanaki. Cornelious knew that with his quick wit and muscular build—he was the track and field coach—Mr.

Chanaki was the lead character in many of his fellow students' daydreams. When Maddie and Cornelious had first taken to running on the boards together, they often passed by Mr. Chanaki on his own daily jog. Cornelious had joked that he finally understood why Maddie enjoyed running so early, whereas Maddie had rolled her eyes and sprinted on ahead of him.

Cornelious walked over to determine if they really had come together, or just happened to be looking like a flawless Spirit of Halloween store ad for couples' costumes. "Good evening Ms. Owens, and uh, Mr. Chanaki."

"Oh, Cornelious," gushed Ms. Owens. He realized it was the first time he had seen her gush, other than when referencing her only son. "Isn't this year's theme so perfect?!"

"Um, yeah. It's great," Cornelious agreed, although he thought quite the opposite. When it was obvious the two weren't going to say anything more, and were stuck gazing into each other's eyes, he ventured in, "So, you two know each other?"

The two adults beamed at each other with such intensity they seemed to morph into star-crossed teenagers. "Actually, I had the good fortune to convince Ms. Owens into being my guest for the evening." As Mr. Chanaki spoke, he reached out and grabbed Ms. Owen's hands, who showed no interest in letting go.

Noticing her son's best friend staring at their interlocked fingers, Ms. Owens giggled and clarified, "We met just this month at Back to School Night. Pilot really loves your class," she finished turning to him.

Cornelious knew that Pilot liked US History as much as he liked licking sandpaper. And although he was not in AP with Maddie and Cornelious, he took Chanaki's regular course, and never mentioned his enthusiasm about it to anyone. But, Cornelious also knew that Jenna Owens did **not** date and tonight she seemed genuinely happy. Grinning broadly Cornelious added, "Yes. He loves technology more than anything so he's hoping to learn about technological advances throughout history."

Mr. Chanaki returned the smile and seemed to deeply consider what his student had said. "Well, we don't get too much into that… but that'd be a good mini-lesson to sneak in at some point."

Cornelious nodded, and left the two in la-la land, as he decided it was time to find his friends. He knew Eric and Jason weren't here tonight, for they had a big game in two days and didn't want to risk devouring candy, or even drinking a little—as Jason had recently decided was cool to do. Therefore, there wasn't much preventing him from seeing his three favorite people in the world. Cornelious skirted away from those obviously wanting to indulge in conversation with him and turned to find his trio huddling in a corner, with a bowl of candy, obviously narrating the scene before them. Cornelious stealthily made his way over, avoiding his father's radar, and jumped right in.

"Did you see Hannah actually dressed as a giant pie?" Carly snickered, motioning to where the blonde girl was awkwardly sitting at a round table.

The gang laughed as Pilot clarified, "She told me that she thought the theme was "Pie, right? It's a treasure!"

5

Fall was officially winding down, as the second week of November was beginning and the cold air seemed intent on staying. Those sports still practicing were lucky or skilled enough to count themselves as contenders in conference playoffs, and hopefully States to follow. Cornelious and Maddie both were eager for their playoff runs to begin and were quite confident in their team's abilities. Although the clear stars of each team, with their reluctance to discuss their individual success (unlike Jason Scott), many teachers forgot the talent they had in their classrooms. This was fine with the duo for, as predisposed as some teachers may be to take it easier on star-athletes, many teachers in Asbury felt the opposite. Whether upset over lack of funding or appreciation, there were some faculty members who had a reputation of increasing the difficulty and amount of work for the whole class when it contained star athletes, such as Mr. McKlien or Mrs. Peri.

Luckily, they never had to worry about receiving such treatment from their previous teacher. As the pair walked down the hall together, on their way from Chanaki's class, playoffs were the only thing on their mind.

"Hey guys, I meant to ask, how was Computers yesterday? I heard Mrs. Dull's husband gave her a Swarovski diamond necklace and she's in a great mood," Carly spilled the latest gossip to her buds as she caught up with them.

Cornelious laughed and realized everything made sense. "So that's why she let us play games the whole class. We were supposed to start our new coding assignment."

Maddie nodded. She knew the bright and bubbly, and rather chubby, computer teacher was always in high spirits—despite the suggestion from her last name—but she thought the teacher was excited for the playoffs to begin as well. After all, Mrs. Dull wasn't always chubby. She used to be a killer field hockey player back in the day.

"Sweet! Now, I have something to look forward to in computers. Usually, Hannah and I just talk anyway but now we won't get in trouble," Carly smiled, and already starting planning all of the juicy gossip she would divulge, and in return, receive from Hannah.

As the trio rounded the corner, Maddie and Cornelious were headed Honors Algebra 2 and Carly to Geometry, they were joined by the Dylans brothers, Bo and Anthony. Anthony, a senior, had been a not-so-secret admirer of Carly Cosentino since Carly started high school last fall. He had even shown up at a few of her Cheer competitions before Pilot worked up the nerve to scare him away. And by scare him away, he simply hacked into his computer and released a virus that only he had the ability to fix. Carly was so impressed with her boyfriend, that she had surprised him with a ticket to the regional 'Wired Weird' convention in Dublin—though she had no clue about anything that was discussed that entire day.

Therefore, Cornelious wasn't too surprised when Anthony slid right next to Carly and made light conversation. What surprised Cornelious, was that his younger brother Bo (a junior and fellow football teammate), had somehow weaseled his way between Cornelious and Maddie and began congratulating her on her season. He knew all her stats and even enthusiastically described some of her top plays. With his background in theater, for he was also a member of the school drama club, Bo's impressions of Maddie's movements were spot on.

For some odd reason, Cornelious felt like a fifth wheel and a pang of anger welled up inside. "Bo, Anthony, nice to see you too," Cornelious cut in. In response, the brothers said hi and waved the trio off, as they headed to their own classes.

As Cornelious and Maddie entered their math class, Cornelious said to Maddie, "I didn't know you were friends with Bo Dylans."

Maddie smirked, "I'm not. He was just being polite."

For some reason, Cornelious thought there was more to it than that; he found he couldn't focus on the elimination method and told himself to relax.

Unfortunately, relaxing in Honors Algebra 2 wasn't such an easy task.

Yet again, Mrs. Gaus had decided to turn today's lesson into a song. Every rule or formula that the petite teacher from Nashville, Tennessee came across was instantly tuned up and cranked out. Even if the students hadn't known she was born and bred in Tennessee, her dark, 1970's Dolly Parton style hair—or her BIG doo, as her former Pre-K kids called it—and deep Southern drawl was proof enough.

After migrating Eastward to Asbury, Mrs. Gaus had been ecstatic to accept the Pre-K job at the primary school. Although quick to create songs and teach through music, many parents complained the lessons were far above their child's mental state. When she was tasked with teaching the basic colors of the rainbow, she became inspired to sing about the light spectrum instead, with all the wavelengths, including the light prism. Luckily, the school district realized they had a wonderful teacher on their hands (as well as wealthy school donor, seeing as her husband is a natural gas tycoon), so they simply moved her to the high school.

To be honest, after her first year, Algebra 2 test scores climbed from twelfth to number one in the state—and have remained there ever since! It seems her songs are too catchy to forget and enable her students to pass virtually every test with flying colors.

Thus, when Cornelious sat behind his best bud, plagued with strange feelings of resentment against Bo Dylans, he found he couldn't stay mad. Not while half the class was jumping around, belting out "Just 'Liminate It' to

the rhythm of Will Smith's 'Gettin' Jiggy With It.'
******

By happy circumstance, both the girls' soccer team and boys' football team had off from practice today. Thus, the gang had an obvious reason to swing by their favorite hangout. After each ordering a various milkshake, and a cookie taco, the gang got caught up—or rather Carly brought her friends up to speed on the latest happenings at Asbury High.

"...and that is why there are so many Ostrich pictures floating around the school," Carly finished, slurping up her milkshake.

Maddie, Pilot, and Cornelious didn't know whether to be nauseated or intrigued, but before any of them could offer anything to the conversation, a good-looking blonde boy, in a turquoise polo and jeans, joined their booth with a smile.

"Hey guys, what's up?" Eric Henry grinned at the group and plopped down right next to Cornelious and directly across from Maddie. Without a second's hesitation he grabbed a fry from Maddie's plate, and threw it in his mouth.

"Hey! That's theft!" Maddie jokingly claimed. Cornelious supposed he should be happy that Eric was now on good terms with his best friends, but every time he listened to Maddie and Eric talk, he found himself wishing Maddie still hated him. Not that he could tell anyone that, nor voice his reasons. Regardless, the thought still lingered, even if he couldn't put a finger on it.

Following Maddie's use of the word theft, the Dylans brothers' heads shot up and looked to the corner booth. Realizing who was sitting there, the brothers got up from their counter seats and made their way over. Not only did the two boys look similar, with brown, short hair and dark brown eyes, but they dressed almost the same too. Carly figured with two kids so close in age and measurements, their mom probably shopped a lot of two-for-one deals. She always knew that neither she nor Mia would ever allow their own mom to do so. Style exists for a reason, and she used it to carve her own separate personality.

"Hey guys, did we hear you mention theft?" Anthony inquired, eyes staring straight at Carly as he spoke.

Taken aback, Maddie answered, "Uh yeah. I was just joking, why what's up?"

The brothers looked at each other, and then Bo slid next to Maddie in the booth. He placed his right arm over her shoulders and then leaned in conspiratorially to the table. Cornelious felt Eric's fists tighten into balls and watched his friend's eyes shrink into slits. Crazy enough, Cornelious knew that the reason being was the location of Bo's arm. Cornelious wanted to tell Eric to relax, and that Maddie wasn't into this bozo, but for the second time today something inside him began to stir as well. Realizing he was eager to hear the Dylans brothers' tale, he pushed away any antagonistic thoughts.

Ensuring he had everyone's rapt attention, and a little confused as to why Eric was glaring at him, he hurriedly explained, "You see, this past weekend, Anthony and I both had about two-thousand dollars robbed right from under our noses!"

Apparently not wanting to miss the limelight, Anthony furthered, “It seems someone withdrew the money from our account, and even had the proper paperwork and knowledge of us to prove to the bank they were legit!”

Maddie’s heart began to race, could this be the start of yet another case? She felt her eyes begin to shine and felt the familiar tug to grab her three best friends and embark on a new mystery. But first, she needed Bo to take his arm off her shoulder. She wasn’t a piece of furniture, after all.

Carly, on the other hand, found herself dreading this news. She had hoped, and even prayed, this year would be a normal teenage year with no cases nor danger. Shaking her head, she realized she should have known better. The only good to come out of this little rendezvous was that Eric had made it perfectly clear just how into her bud he really was. Thinking of possible fun double dates, Carly hoped that Maddie would realize this and give Eric the chance he so desperately wanted.

Pilot was too busy trying to decipher the look on his girlfriend’s face. He knew she wasn’t exactly fond of their adventures, but he also knew a part of her loved solving the mysteries they always found themselves involved in. He turned his attention back to the conversation, and realized, with glee, that this case could prove to be rather technological, as it involved a large amount of money and a financial institution. Rubbing his hands together under the table, Pilot envisioned the program he could create to worm his way into the bank’s security, undetected.

Cornelious heard the sob story and thought the brothers were living it up. They may have been robbed, but they clearly just wanted attention, and the longer Bo had his arm around Maddie the more Cornelious was sure of it.

"I kind of blame myself in a way," Bo added sadly, shaking his head in anguish.

In a voice full of malice, Eric was quick to agree. "Yeah, you probably gave your passwords away." Eric was also wondering the quickest way to discreetly rip Bo away from Maddie, but could think of no possible way without freaking Maddie out. He had just gotten on good terms with her and wasn't about to mess that up.

"No, nothing like that," Anthony defended his brother. "Bo jammed his finger at football practice and had to take off his lucky ring."

Cornelious wanted to ask how a bench-warmer jammed his finger but realized how mean that sounded. He was ashamed, for he never claimed to be better than anyone and knew how hard it was to play a high school sport. He wondered where these feelings were coming from, and was distracted as the brothers left the table, claiming they had work to do.

Before the five of them could discuss what the Dylans had just divulged, a cute (or conniving, if you ask Maddie) red-headed girl and her absent-minded but pretty, blonde-headed best friend strolled over to their table.

"Hey guys! What was that about, Maddie? Are you and Bo an item?" Alexis asked innocently.

Maddie and Cornelious choked on their milkshake, and Carly smiled knowingly. Pilot asked the obvious, as he had no clue what Alexis meant. Surely, he would know if Maddie was dating anyone. They weren't just best friends, but neighbors as well. "What are you talking about?"

Alexis batted her eyelashes and held up both hands

in defense, "Oh. I'm sorry, it looked like Bo Dylans was getting cozy with you. That's all."

"Yeah, it looked like he was your boyfriend," Hannah clarified.

"Well, he definitely is not. I barely know the kid," Maddie protested, knowing that Hannah spoke the plain, and often times, way simple truth. With playoffs coming up, she didn't want to have to contend with a dumb high school rumor as well. After her freshman year, she felt that she had more than her fair share of gossip.

"Yeah, he's not her type," Cornelious slipped out, not meaning to say anything but feeling unable to contain himself.

Maddie looked at him strangely, and Carly's grin grew wider.

"And what is her type?" Eric questioned innocently.

"Yeah, what is my type?" Maddie leaned across the table towards her best friend, who began to blush.

Luckily, Cornelious was saved from having to answer by the one who started them on this path.

"Not important," Alexis declared. "What is important, is that I'm in charge of making your playoff goodie basket. We just started doing that this year... I was wondering, what your favorite cookies are. I know you like sweet things." Alexis winked, and both Carly and Maddie silently gagged. Everyone knew Alexis was obsessed with Cornelious Gibbz. Maddie was just glad Cornelious didn't seem to reciprocate the feelings.

But when he smiled up at her and said anything chocolate will do, Maddie wasn't so sure Cornelious wasn't charmed by her nemesis. Plus, she thought, he wouldn't like a chocolate lemon cookie, thinking back to when Sophia had baked them a variety of cookies a few years back. After devouring all of them, they ended with a yellowish-brown cookie. The second they swallowed the final cookie, they both raced outside to throw up the chocolatey-lemon flavor.

Alexis giggled and told Cornelious to text her anytime if he had anything particular in mind, or even to chat about nothing at all.

Cornelious blushed, again, and the two girls left Brady's with a little pep in their step. Hannah couldn't have told you why, but Alexis felt she was well on the way to becoming Cornelious Gibbz' girlfriend.

6

A few minutes after the departure of Alexis and Hannah, Eric felt as if the quartet wished to discuss what they just learned, privately. He understood. These four had been inseparable for years and taking into account all they had accomplished the past year alone it was no small wonder that no one had dubbed them the next A-Team… yet. Standing up, Eric again considered how lucky Cornelious was to get to hang around Maddie Petrozza as often as he wanted. He knew that her parents even let him sleepover in her room! Fortunately, Eric knew there was no romantic feelings between the two, or surely, they'd be like Carly and Pilot by now. Smiling at the reassurance, he checked his watch, and bid the foursome goodbye.

The gang only waited about five minutes after Eric had left to pay their bill (greatly discounted for all they had done for Brady's this past summer). Leaving the restaurant, they couldn't believe their good fortune, as the trolley was parked at the bottom of the ramp. Grateful not to have to run after it for once, Pilot slowly stepped up onto the trolley and walked over to a pair of open seats. Gesturing for Carly to sit inside (for he knew she loved the window seat), he quickly took his spot next to her, as she leaned over and kissed him on the cheek. Opting to stand at the rear and hold onto the rail, Cornelious and Maddie watched their friends, holding hands and whispering quietly, and smiled.

As they neared Pilot and Maddie's neighborhood, the group jumped off and hurried to Pilot's room. Even for those who had never been in Pilot's room—which outside of those currently in attendance, left just his own mother—it wouldn't be too difficult for others to visualize it. Pilot was known to all as a slightly strange, albeit technological God. It would therefore surprise no one the ferocity in which he fortified his room. In addition to a sound-proof door, Pilot had a private self-made P.A. system, so he would know who wished to enter. If the visitor failed to speak into the gray box on the wall, Pilot had also installed multiple, undetectable cameras throughout his house. Thus, making it possible for him to monitor even when he was not home.

Once the gang had entered his room, Maddie and Cornelious were shocked to see that his usual whirlwind of gadgets and gizmos strewn across every available space, was rather orderly. Maddie couldn't remember ever seeing the wooden floor before and bent down to make sure it wasn't a hologram or some other technological mirage.

"It's real," Maddie whispered to Cornelious, who was shocked into silence.

"I know how nervous Pilot makes you guys when we're in here," Carly beamed. "So, I worked with him to organize and categorize his tech." She turned to face her boyfriend, "You have to admit it makes finding things a lot easier, and there's more room for us to hang out."

Pilot smiled. Once again, looking at Carly's beautiful smile, he considered himself the luckiest guy in the world. If he had known sooner that she wanted to hang out (alone with him) in his room more, he would've tossed everything out of the window. Or at least, have pushed everything in the corner. Even though, he admitted to himself, her system of cleanliness was an even better solution.

"Okay lovebirds," Maddie broke in as the two looked at each unabashed, "Let's get down to business."

Carly grinned again and sat on the edge of Pilot's uncharacteristically clean bed. Maddie and Cornelious (who felt he could breathe for once, as Pilot's room induced fear deep in his core), sat down next to each other at the foot of the bed. "You two will be happy with this."

Pilot, trying to look nonchalant, joined Carly at the end of his bed and spoke the words: "Mystery, begin."

Without warning, the lights dimmed and a projector slid out from the ceiling. A program opened that read clear as day: CASE 3.

Maddie turned to grin at Pilot. "You created a program for us to solve mysteries?" Her voice was full of awe. No more hand cramps for her!

Pilot smiled sheepishly, "I know we have always done pen and paper, or marker and easel. But after this summer's poisonings, I realized that although we were lucky you can write so quick, just imagine how much easier it would be to dictate. Thus, I invented the Mystery Machine."

Cornelious laughed, "Like, from Scooby Doo?"

"Exactly! Who better to draw inspiration from than a group of friends solving crimes?"

No one could argue, and the group took turns recording their voices so the program would only respond to them. Pilot explained that they could say "Mystery Machine record in" whatever section they wished to add information. As of now, they had no suspects nor any clues, so Pilot suggested they utilize the Mystery Machine debate section. Here, they could talk about everything they knew and the program would sum everything up nicely. However, they could choose to keep a separate file of the original debate, in case the computer missed something. After all, sometimes the smallest thing—such as the act of missing your Senior Prom—can break a case.

"Okay, so the next step should be to look at the bank's security footage and begin monitoring online activity," Pilot stated.

"That sounds like a job you were made for," Cornelious responded, knowing only Pilot had the know-how to complete both tasks.

******

The weekend before Thanksgiving Break, both the Asbury girls' soccer team and the boys' football team ended their seasons. Last year, both teams had made it to the state semifinals and both teams had lost. As if they were made to mirror each other, yet again, both teams had found their way to the Finals. Unfortunately for Cornelious and

Maddie, who vowed to never miss each other's game when they could help it, their State Championship games were scheduled for the same day, and only two hours apart.

Therefore, they wished each other luck, boarded their busses, and went their separate ways. Even more unfortunate, was that both teams had lost in overtime—with Maddie's defeat coming in the form of penalty kicks. Losing on penalty kicks was as heart-wrenching as Rose losing Jack on the Titanic. And it made about as much sense. After fighting a long battle, why not just extend the time and keep fighting on until someone scores—or in Jack's case swim on to another floating object?

When both buses of defeated teams had made their way home to Asbury, it was only about six o'clock in the evening. Carly, coming off the cheerleading bus, announced to her friends that the Hestons had given Hannah permission to throw a party—tonight! Apparently, the cheerleaders had already planned every aspect on their drive home, so there was little else to do besides spread the word.

Maddie looked at her friends wearily. The last thing she wanted to do tonight was celebrate. They had come within inches of winning a state championship and had failed. She wanted to wallow in her loss, and then vow to never feel this way again.

Sensing her friends' opposition to party, Carly put her pom poms to her hips and declared, "Come on, guys! You know how many teams don't even make it to the playoffs—and we went all the way!"

When neither Cornelious nor Maddie showed any signs of excitement, Carly pouted. "Pilot won't come if it's just me going."

Although that may or may not have been true, Cornelious knew how nervous Pilot would be, and relented. "Alright, let me change. She lives down the road from me, so you guys can just meet me outside my gates." Cornelious would have invited them in, but didn't want them to endure a roasting from his father. Which they all pretty much understood.

Maddie though, not one for parties, held her ground. "I'm not into it," and she held up her hand to silence her friends before they could lodge a complaint. "And I already told Milton that this weekend I would catch up on Cunningham's book club with him. I guess I'd rather get it over with tonight then spend tomorrow doing it."

Carly grumbled that Maddie needed to branch out and be a teenager for once, but Cornelious understood this would be a good way to distract herself from her loss. Plus, he found himself thinking, it's just Milton she'll be with. He didn't know why, but that thought made him smile.

As they separated, Maddie further consoled herself by remembering that Milton's father, Wolfgang, was the premier German Butcher in the country. She would at least have a happy stomach tonight.

A few hours later, the majority of Asbury High's teenagers had clustered in the expansive mansion of Hannah Heston. Although Carly, Pilot, and Cornelious had not started drinking alcohol yet, some of their peers had, and cheap beer and wine were readily within reach. The Hestons figured that if the kids wanted to drink, they might as well do it from the safety of their home. Anyone who reached for a red cup had to first deposit their keys, if they were of driving age.

The second Cornelious walked in the door, he was grabbed by Alexis Johnson. Still wearing her cheerleading outfit (as were all of the cheerleaders, as they deemed this party was only happening to show Aces pride), she immediately laced her arm through his, and jabbered away about how great his season was, and that next year they'd win for sure and he'd definitely be named MVP. During her onslaught of compliments, which left his ego more inflated than a hot air balloon, he glanced up and made eye contact with fellow teammate Jason Scott. Jason, ever the image-man, had a beer in each hand and a girl on each arm. He also donned his Varsity letter jacket and nodded to Cornelious giving him two thumbs up in approval.

Approval for the season? Or coming to the party? Cornelious considered, but realizing this was Jason Scott he was considering, understood it was most likely because he had Alexis Johnson on his arm. Still weary of how his last 'crush/party-date' had been, Cornelious nonchalantly looked over Alexis. With her naturally red curly hair, reaching a little past her shoulders, and flawless skin, Alexis was very pretty. Lately, she genuinely seemed to be trying to be nice. Or at least nicer.

Plus, Cornelious discovered how nice it felt to have someone constantly complimenting him and making him feel important. He further knew this was no basis for a relationship, but he sure as heck wasn't looking for one. Cornelious scanned the room and found Pilot and Carly were huddled in a corner surrounded by Hannah and some other jocks. He knew that though they enjoyed spending all their time together and made dating seem rather nice,

Cornelious couldn't imagine wanting to be alone with someone that often.

Alexis, on the other hand, looked up at her prize, and felt pretty soon she'd be half of the new it couple.

As the night droned on, party games were introduced, and Cornelious and Carly were surprised that Pilot was very good at beer pong. Of course, he played with water while his partner, Eric, did the drinking. However, Pilot hit his mark so often, even Eric barely drank.

After their latest string of six consecutive wins, Pilot took a break to find Carly. Hannah stopped him and put her hands on his chest, saying she never knew how good he was a pong-pong. He smiled, thanked her, and went to his girlfriend, who was sitting next to Cornelious on the back of a couch.

"Seems you caught our hostess' eye," Carly half-joked.

"Hannah? She's just being nice. Plus, she's in all my classes this year, so we've become… friends, I guess." Pilot shrugged, and turned back to wave at Hannah, who was still staring him.

Cornelious checked his phone and realized it was getting late—almost midnight. "Hey guys, should we get going? I bet Maddie is done her book club, and I wanted to check in with her… she did have her team's lone goal of the game, and I don't even think I congratulated her."

Carly smiled and snuggled into Pilot's side. "Well, if she isn't done, then they're doing more than reading," Pilot joked.

Cornelious whipped his head to face Pilot, but Eric interrupted.

"Maddie's at a book club? Tonight? On a Saturday?" Eric looked incredulous. "That explains why she wasn't here."

Carly answered, "No, she's not here because she hates parties and drunks. Even though I tell her half the kids don't even drink."

Eric nodded, and wiped his hand back across his hair. "Well, tell her she was missed… and maybe don't mention I drank then."

Carly smiled knowingly and said she would. Before Cornelious could respond, Carly grabbed the boys' hands and headed out the door. She stopped on the doorstep and faced Cornelious. "Do you want to, um, say bye to Alexis?"

Confused, he answered, "No. Why? I'll see her Monday."

Shaking her head, she waved him off and quickly threw herself aside as Ed and Jason came running out the door shirtless, but covered in red lipstick that clearly spelled 'Aces' across each boy's chest. Boys, Carly thought to herself, as she straightened up and left the party with her two buds, arm in arm.

7

Cornelious had grown up a Gibbz. In all meanings of the word. For most people, holidays were a time of quiet celebration or loud get-togethers with family and friends. Even the most boring of holidays are filled with memories and positivity. For years, Cornelious had enviously listened to each of his three friends detail the craziness and warmth that made up their holidays. Even the tamer celebrations sounded as if they were still family-oriented.

For the Gibbz family, of Jeremiah, Nancy, and Cornelious, the holidays were a time to boast about their good fortune. Thus, these days proved an optimum time for photo ops and good publicity. Adding to their nuclear family, was Cornelious' one-time favorite cousin (because only recently had his curly-headed cousin gotten under his skin), Dane. Because Dane was now a member of his private high school's prestigious golf team (which ran throughout the entire school year), he had little time to spend in Asbury this Thanksgiving. However, as Jeremiah proudly told his wife and son, Dane had refused to miss Jeremiah's first Thanksgiving as Mayor.

Stepping out of his private helicopter in his perfectly pressed Burberry winter coat, and navy-blue pants, Dane wrapped his cousin in a bear hug, and greeted his Aunt in a similar fashion. As for his Uncle, he made sure to square his shoulders, and extend his hand for a strong, power-filled handshake. Accepting the gesture with gleaming eyes, Cornelious rolled his eyes and watched the helicopter take off again, from its landing spot in his own backyard. Why waste time driving into Mainland for their public airport when the Gibbz estate was so large?

The Gibbz trio, plus Dane (who was not a Gibbz, as he was Nancy's sister's boy), were making their way down to the West side in their luxurious, private limo. As Nancy Gibbz stared absentmindedly at her perfectly manicured hands—with a little turkey drawn on each nail--Cornelious wondered what his mother was actually thinking. Only a year ago he thought she was good-natured, but rather vapid. But when his best friend's mother had needed help the most, Nancy Gibbz, an unlikely heroine as ever, swooped in with the bird-like family attorney, and effectively saved the day. Thinking back, Cornelious was ashamed to think that he had never actually thanked his mother, but wasn't sure where to start now. Most conversations with his mom had centered around topics of herself or monetary value, or even her beloved fat cat Howie. To all of which he wasn't an eager conversationalist.

"I just don't know which one is more…more…"

began Jeremiah Gibbz, as he compared two brown ties that looked exactly the same, but apparently had some microscopic differences.

"Appropriate, dear?" Nancy offered, still inspecting her manicure.

"Not exactly, my love. I was thinking of…"

Tilting his head, Dane inquired, "Festive?"

"No… not that either…" Jeremiah exhaled, holding the ties even closer to his eyes.

"Powerful," Cornelious muttered, choosing to stare out the window, rather than make eye contact with his father.

Jeremiah's broad grin lit up the back seat, "Exactly, my boy! You are learning the lingo."

Even Dane, who was sitting right next to Cornelious, smacked his cousin proudly on the knee.

Cornelious sighed and told his father the one in his right hand looked more imposing. Not realizing his son was joking, Jeremiah proudly chose the one in his right, and settled back into a state of comfort and serenity. Or as close to it as the imposing Mayor/Governor could get in the back of a limo.

As they neared the soup kitchen, Cornelious pictured the rest of the day with full clarity. Dane would be snuggled up close to Jeremiah, vying for his attention, while storing away mental notes on succeeding in politics, or the wealthy-life in general, he supposed. By the end of the night, his face would hurt from smiling for the ever-snapping camera, and his stomach would be as empty as JB's brain.

When the handsome family exited the cab,

Cornelious' mother surprised him for a second time. "We are only staying here until five." Checking his wristwatch, he saw, to his horror, it was ten am. His mother continued, whispering in his ear, "I told your father you had plans with the Cosentinos for dinner, but I arranged for Julio to drive you to Maddie's."

With that, Nancy straightened up, smiled, and led her surprised son into the soup kitchen.

For once, the Gibbzs were on the same side of town as the Petrozzas and Owens during Thanksgiving, but for Cornelious it seemed as if he were a million miles away.

At the Petrozza home, Sophia was enjoying total control of the remote, and kept switching between various parades and E! Hollywood News updates. Trent and Alec were outside with the twins, tossing around a football, but secretly distracting Daniel and Shannon from their mission to add their beloved red sauce to each dish. Mrs. Petrozza was busying herself by putting on finishing touches and seemingly intensifying the succulent aromas which each move. Joining her, and adding some much-needed adult conversation, as well as spreading her homemade-turkey-dinner-in-each-state tablecloth, was Ms. Owens. This year Mrs. Petrozza was especially pleased, for her longtime neighbor and dear friend, had actually brought a date to Thanksgiving! And an extremely good-looking, young man too, thought Mrs. Petrozza. Apparently, he was even Maddie's teacher—something Mrs. Petrozza found interesting and vowed to pull some more information from her oldest daughter later.

For once Mr. Petrozza found himself enjoying conversation with another adult male on Thanksgiving (both Petrozzas were so busy with kids and full-time self-employment that they rarely had time for adult conversation). Andrew Chanaki, as Jenna Owens' guest introduced himself, was quick-witted, and funny, not to mention clearly athletic. Obviously, he should have been a favorite of Maddie's, but Mr. Petrozza couldn't remember his daughter ever mentioning him. Though, she had been busy with schoolwork and soccer playoffs, and tomorrow's tryouts! His kids sure were busy and Mr. Petrozza couldn't have been prouder.

Despite the belief that children of single parents automatically dislike their parent's choice of date, Pilot was genuinely happy for his mom. Being a romantic himself, for he had loved Carly Cosentino from the moment he had laid eyes on her, he often wished his mom would find such happiness. And although he was sure some of his peers would poke fun at his mom dating his teacher, he couldn't care less. No one could ever accuse Pilot Owens of being a suck-up or teacher's pet—at least not in history class.

While the food was cooking, Pilot found himself sitting out on the front porch with Maddie beside him, and La telling an animated tale about her most recent adventure in Peru with a llama-wrangler, an anaconda and a bucket of fresh tar. Even though La might not be getting any younger, she sure was not slowing down. Neither Maddie nor Pilot doubted any aspect of her retelling. For although her stories may seem outrageous, they nonetheless proved true. Every single time.

Thanksgiving at the Petrozzas was an all-day affair. Beginning with a saliva-inducing brunch around eleven, and a few appetizers throughout, the main course usually wasn't served any earlier than 4:30. Therefore, a little after five, the Owens and Petrozzas, with the addition of Andrew Chanaki, were just sitting down to their long-awaited meal, when a well-dressed teenager came bounding through the door, pulling a chair in from the porch and sliding in right next to his best friend.

"Neal?" Maddie questioned, knowing his day was spent at the soup kitchen.

Cornelious grinned, "My mom said she talked to your mom, and actually had Julio drop me off after we finished at the kitchen."

Mrs. Owens returned a warm smile, "That is correct. Apparently, your parents are eating their dinner at your Aunt's house and are flying out of town tonight."

So that's why Dane hadn't brought a suitcase, Cornelious realized. Though clearly unaware of this arrangement, he wasn't disturbed. He was used to being on his own and knew he would crash at Maddie's if this was the case.

"Dane was here?" Maddie asked, looking at Cornelious.

Cornelious raked his hand back through his hair, "Yeah, he wanted to witness my dad's first Thanksgiving as Mayor, or something like that… and he wanted me to tell you he says hi and he misses you… or something like that."

Maddie grinned, and pictured Cornelious' well-dressed, crazy cousin following Jeremiah around the soup kitchen with a notebook and pen, poised to take notes.

Cornelious didn't know why mentioning Dane would make Maddie smile, but he knew of his cousin's inclination to flirt with his best friend, and wasn't too pleased.

"Anyway, I'm here now, and ready to eat!" Cornelious proclaimed, surveying the table. Everyone laughed and agreed it was time to dive in.

Maddie smiled, "Well, good. But don't think you can eat all the green bean casserole, that's my favorite dish too!"

"I'm surprised you two can eat all," Trent, an athlete himself, shook his head in disbelief. "If I had basketball tryouts tomorrow, I'd be too nervous to eat."

Cornelious and Maddie grinned at each other, while Pilot read their minds.

"Those two are machines. They don't get nervous."

8

After a long weekend of devouring leftovers for most people, and sprinting and drills for a select few, Monday morning sprang up on the gang with exciting news.

The hallways were buzzing with news of yet another theft. Students and teachers could be found clustering up between classes, eagerly swapping news of the latest crime to hit Asbury. Even evil Janitor Cutro was pleased, for he now had a valid excuse to hit the Achilles and/or ankles of anyone in his path as he was 'clearing' the hallways. With a new season just beginning, Cornelious and Maddie kept a keen eye out for the hunched over, wrinkly old janitor, who was as stealthy as a Navy Seal in his prime.

With all the noise and gossip spreading around, it was (naturally) Carly who revealed the truth to the gang, following lunch. Apparently, the Hunters, a large family from the West Side, had reported that their savings of nearly five thousand dollars had been withdrawn from their bank account! The bank had no explanation other than someone in the family had taken the money out from their account over the weekend at some point, but each member claimed total innocence and/or ignorance.

"This is some serious déjà vu from last year," Carly moaned, shutting her locker and turning to face her friends.

Maddie shook her head in disagreement, "Other than money being stolen, there doesn't seem to be any similarities."

"How so? This is only the second case we've heard about…if you even believe the Dylans brothers' story." Cornelious muttered, looking around for Cutro's yellow cart.

Maddie looked over her friends in disbelief. They had another case unfolding in front of them, and they all seemed less than eager to investigate. "Guys, look at the thefts. Both times, the money was withdrawn straight from the bank AND it's not just the wealthy getting ripped off this time either."

Pilot beamed and rose his fist on the air, "Looks like it's time for the Mystery Machine!"

Maddie agreed, and Carly grabbed Pilot's balled fist and pulled it back down to Earth, laughing.

"Okay," Cornelious sighed, still unwilling to believe the Dylans, but acknowledging the Hunters wouldn't have fabricated a story, seeing as they surely needed the money with their big family. "I agree we should look everything over, and record our thoughts… didn't you say you would monitor banking and online activity?"

Cornelious questioned his tech-savvy friend.

Before Pilot could reply, the bell rang beckoning students to their classes, mirroring cattle drawn to their stalls.

Cornelious and Maddie waved goodbye to their other half and headed into their History class with Mr. Chanaki.

"I hope this isn't awkward since he was just in your house this Thanksgiving," Cornelious whispered as the pair took their seats. The only thing worse than a mean teacher, was one who thought they were your best friend.

Maddie smiled and added, "He did come by later on the next day too, and helped with chores."

"Seriously?" Cornelious asked incredulously. He slid in his seat, right behind Maddie in the center of the room, and pictured how quickly the track and field coach would be able to accomplish a cleaning task. In his mind, he saw Chanaki as a cartoon character, who finished in a huff, leaving the Petrozza household sparkling.

Maddie laughed and spun to face the front, where the word: **CULTS** was sprawled out across the board in bold lettering. She was about to turn around and remark to Cornelious how awesome today's class should be (the two of them had loved studying cults and watching film on the Discovery Channel for years now), when she caught Alexis' green-eyed glare shooting daggers at her from across the room. However, Alexis' expression changed from murderous to welcoming so fast, Maddie half-convinced herself that she had imagined it. In fact, Alexis offered a small wave and swiftly faced the board, leaving Maddie's mind whirling. Tread carefully, Maddie warned herself. Although Alexis had offered a parley the other day, Maddie wasn't so easily fooled and knew to stay on guard.

"Cults!" boomed their handsome History teacher as he strode into the room. In addition to being good-looking and well-liked, Andrew Chanaki was known to drop random facts on his students daily. Many students claimed they would easily win Jeopardy, after a year in his class. "Usually defined as a relatively small group of people having religious beliefs or practices regarded by others as strange or sinister. Or at times a small group's misguided **excessive** admiration of a particular person or thing." Mr. Chanaki stopped to let the class soak up the definition and play it over in their young minds before proceeding. "Of course, many of us tend to think of cults as a bunch of crazies running around and getting others to do their evil biddings. And unfortunately, most times the only cults that get remembered or widely-acclaimed are those considered, well, evil. In fact, there are numerous cults practicing today, in which you may never hear about, and some which will—undoubtedly—make sad or sickening headlines."

Cornelious, sitting behind Maddie as he tended to do when he was unable to sit next to her, smiled when he saw his best friend was literally on the edge of her seat. It took him a second, but he chuckled as he realized he was as well.

"Today we will discuss the most famous, perhaps sinister, yet somewhat unknown cults in American His—" the door suddenly sprung open, successfully cutting off their teacher's lesson and revealing a sinister figure they all unfortunately knew about.

The imposing bald man stepped into the classroom

and scanned the room as if his Bluetooth earpiece (which never left his ear), had possessed laser-shooting abilities and he was in the process of searching for a target to decimate. In Maddie and Cornelious' experience, he very well could have installed such technology over the summer.

"Good afternoon Principal Coste," Mr. Chanaki welcomed his boss into the room.

"I'll make this short and to the point," Mr. Coste snarled. "Last year two of our own were responsible for irresponsibly wreaking havoc on this town. Rest assured no faculty member will ever dare venture into students' lives the way Ms. Clarke did… however, I am warning all the students to focus on academia during the school hours here. And nothing else. If I hear of any gossip about a student and teacher relationship, even if it is in jest, be certain I will take severe action and the student will not be seen nor heard from again."

Maddie and Cornelious had no need to verbalize their thoughts to each other. A quick glance into the other's face revealed they were thinking the same thought: Was Coste threatening to expel them or murder them?

As if it were meant to be, not only did both Varsity basketball teams schedule practice at the same time, but they also decided to let them out at five-thirty sharp. Therefore, Maddie and Cornelious found themselves walking the boardwalk after practice, reliving various drills and parts of their practice to each other. Cornelious' impression of Baruff, his small yet raucous Italian coach, was spot on. Even his accent sounded first generation Italian. Although Maddie couldn't give as good of an impersonation of Coach Willy, she explained how he had made them scrimmage five on four—with there always being an extra defender, similar to playing with a steady quarterback in flag football. She had to admit it made them work even harder to score, although her very talented teammate Nya managed to do so almost every other possession.

The duo passed by Brady's, but found they weren't hungry, and without much homework to do, they kept walking and talking. As they neared the end of the boardwalk, Cornelious pointed over to the ramp saying, "Isn't that Officer Chip?"

Maddie looked over to where he was pointing and her eyes lit up like a Christmas tree. "Yes! Let's go ask him about the Hunters!"

Cornelious was going to argue that it probably wasn't such a good idea to involve themselves—or to let the cops know they were involving themselves—but he felt himself being literally dragged over to where the new Police Chief stood. He had learned from years of experience that when Maddie wanted something bad enough, it was best to go along with it.

As the friends neared their favorite officer in town (it's a short list), they quieted themselves when they realized he was speaking rapidly into his cell. "Yes. Yes sir, I know. It's all over every news channel as breaking news… no… no… I have no reason to believe… okay… okay sir. Thank you." Chip hung up, and gracefully turned to face Maddie and Cornelious.

Seeing who it was, the newly-appointed Chief of Police whistled out a low breath and massaged his temples. "Now this?" he asked to himself, "What is it?"

Cornelious was all for letting Maddie take the lead here, as it was her idea in the first place. She gracefully released her hold on his sleeve and brought her hands together in a sweet gesture (or at least she hoped it appeared that way).

"First off, let me congratulate you. Chief of Police! Congrats! You're really coming up in the world." Maddie smiled sweetly and placed a hand on Chip's shoulder.

Grunting in reply, "You know, you're touching an officer of the law, right?"

Realizing that in this situation, kindness wasn't king, Maddie rapidly withdrew her hand as if she has placed it on the stovetop. "Okay, so clearly not one for compliments… got it… so, um… sir, how are things?" Maddie inquired, dropping her hands but still smiling like an angel.

Tired of the small talk already, and having loads on his plate, as he was indeed the new Asbury Police Chief, Chip tapped his toes and ignored the teen's angelic act. "Before I shoo you, let's get to the point. What is this about?"

Crossing her arms, Maddie stared Chip in the eyes and began, "We wanted to talk to you about the breaking news."

Chip's eyes shrunk into slits as he squinted at the two teens. "You two know something about the Prison Break?"

Maddie and Cornelious exchanged confused glances. There was no prison in Asbury, and escaping inmates were the furthest thing from their minds.

Chip misread their expressions and further pressed

on, "I don't know how you guys always find yourselves in the middle of every investigation, but this is no joke. If you know something about how the youngest Boni brother managed to help his two brothers escape from their maximum-security prison in New York, you have to spill. This is a matter of national—even inter-national security."

Understanding his best friend better than even himself, he knew Maddie was speechless. Thus, he decided to speak up, "Ummm, no. We were actually going to ask if there have been any leads in the Dylans and Hunters missing money."

Chief Chip's face fell in either relief or disappointment. It was hard to tell. "I'm going to say this once. Stay out of active—or even inactive—police investigations."

Maddie, snapping back to herself, saluted Chip and valiantly answered, "Yes, sir!" She then slid her arm into Cornelious' and steered him away from Chip's searching eyes.

After they were a block away from Chip, Maddie whispered frantically. "Oh my gosh! A prison break! And the Boni brothers!"

"How do I know that name?" Cornelious asked looking sideways at Maddie. But Maddie was lost in her own world and gripping tightly to his arm. Part of him wanted to disengage himself from his friend's death grip, for fear of loss of circulation. But another part of him, realized he liked her holding his arm so tight. The latter thought filled Cornelious with a strange sense of nervousness, leading him to quickly step back and release himself.

Seemingly unaware, Maddie turned to face Cornelious and explained, “The Boni brothers were those criminals that the Cosentinos helped imprison with their photographs, remember?”

Vaguely remembering and eager to distract himself, he inquired, “What does this have to do with us?”

Maddie shrugged, “Probably nothing. Apparently, they literally just escaped, as it’s breaking news and all.... But still it’s exciting!”

“I bet Mr. and Mrs. Cosentino don’t think so.” Cornelious stated.

Maddie considered this and shrugged, “I’m pretty sure Mr. Cosentino said their names were left out of their deposition and testimony, to protect their family.”

“Oh. Well, I know my dad would be putting the estate in lockdown.” Cornelious laughed, “he probably is now anyway.”

Maddie stopped walking and suddenly beamed up at Cornelious. “Hey! At least we got another good piece of information from Chip.”

When it was clear Maddie wanted further prodding from Cornelious he asked, “And what exactly might that be?”

“He said to stay out of police investigations...which is basically admitting there is a case underway for the missing bank money.”

Cornelious grinned and felt that finally, his sophomore year was truly beginning.

9

Upon learning that there was a national manhunt for the escaped convict brothers, not much had changed in the small town of Asbury. Even the town news station chose to run a story on a colony of seagulls that could harmonize on command, rather than report on the prison break.

Besides, just as Maddie predicted, Carly and her family weren't concerned. Carly even assured the gang that any updates on the Bonis would immediately be brought to her parents' attention. This was due to their high-profile friends, deep within various security agencies—both public and private. To which Pilot secretly reminded himself never to anger Miles or Megan Cosentino.

Nevertheless, Maddie and Cornelious rushed to Pilot's to discuss the breakout and their conversation with good ole' Chip. Even the projected wait outside of Pilot's room couldn't break their stride. After two minutes of verifying their identification, they were allowed access.

The two excitedly burst in the room, rambling a mile a minute. Carly, impressed with her friends' gossip, lounged back on Pilot's bed with her head on his lap. Listening to Cornelious and Maddie share the gossip for once, she smirked up at Pilot, happy to finally be rubbing off on them. Pilot smiled back, and pulled out his handy universal remote, enabling a projector to come sliding out from his ceiling. "Mystery, commence."

Cornelious and Maddie hurriedly scrambled onto Pilot's bed, and excitedly sat at the edge.

"We were just talking about when you two would bring up the bank robberies," Carly explained knowingly, "and Pilot's been keeping a running tab on the bank's security both online and from the security cameras located inside of the bank."

Cornelious laughed, "We should've known."

Pilot smiled in return, but then let out a disappointed breath of air. "It's the same as last time, I'm afraid. There is zero fraudulent or suspicious online activity, and some accounts have no activity at all—which no, Maddie, is not suspicious because some people still don't trust the internet enough to bank online and prefer to do everything in person."

Maddie, who was about to interrupt as Pilot surmised, closed her mouth and sat back down—her mind working at ultra-speed.

"And... Pilot and I looked over the bank's security footage and there's nothing out of the ordinary there. In fact, it seems like the people who claim their money is missing, came in and withdrew the money themselves! Or had a close relative do it—with identity and security confirmation." Carly further revealed.

Cornelious turned to his friends, "So everyone who is reporting missing money is either lying or forgetful? That doesn't seem possible…. thousands of dollars is a lot of money to misplace."

Maddie agreed, "Heck, I'm pissed when I lose twenty bucks… although, it's usually Sophia taking it for a 'mall detox'."

Carly shook her head knowingly, while the boys looked incredulous. "That's a thing?" Cornelious asked.

"Apparently," Maddie shrugged.

"That's a stupid thing then," Pilot muttered.

"I don't know… she's such a girly girl and lives with all of you… it probably helps her decompress," Carly said.

"She's in fifth grade… what does she need to decompress?" Maddie skeptically inquired.

Carly sighed and said never mind, it was clear they weren't going to agree on this point. However, the gang did agree there was something fishy going on over at Asbury Bank and they were determined to figure it out.

******

In schools across America, the day before Christmas break is always filled with hope and joy. And in most high schools, there is also the usual drama. With some couples calling it quits before the break (possibly to avoid buying presents or getting in too deep with someone), plans for festive parties getting revealed, and Christmas goodies being exchanged, the student body was fueled by drama and sugar. For most teachers, a large dose of patience, good humor and coffee was prescribed, and although it was a half day, it couldn't seem to end soon enough.

Maddie, Carly, and Cornelious were standing in the lunch line—along with virtually every other student. For the day before the holiday break, Brady's always supplied the cafeteria with a delicious and semi-nutritious lunch menu. Although Pilot's mom had packed him lunch, his friends promised to share and he volunteered to save them a seat (as the lunches were condensed from four lunches to two, and it was already bursting at the seams).

The trio were discussing the current success of both the boys' and girls' basketball teams. As usual Baruff's tough, but hilarious ways were described in detail, as well as Willy's natural good-humor. Their discussion of coaching led them to talk about Mainland's coaching problems this year, as the parents were essentially running the school. And even though they all detested Mainland, it was frustrating to hear that parents were critiquing the coaches and calling them after each game to complain about playing time and how the coaches should speak to their children. This whole idea that coaches need to be friendly or nice to their players angered Maddie and Cornelious. Sports were supposed to teach life lessons, and too many parents got involved when they shouldn't. After all, it was high school. The best kids will play, and if your kid isn't the best it's obvious. Just another reason to be glad that Asbury School District had implanted a no parent-involvement mandate in regards to coaching and sports. After all, with parents always doing everything for their kids and not letting them learn to fail or stand up for themselves, what kind of future are they giving them?

In the midst of their discussion, Eric had joined them and added his two cents, "Yeah, last year when I was upset I was only on the freshmen roster for football, my parents told me if I was that upset I needed to talk to the coach myself and ask what I can do better and THEN practice every single day."

Grabbing a carton of milk, Maddie smiled, "It sounds like you have good parents."

"Well, you met my chatty mom already… you can come over to meet my dad whenever you'd like," Eric blushed, and reached for a plate of Brady's to load onto his tray.

Cornelious turned his head to look over his friends, and saw Carly smiling to herself. Maddie shrugged and replied, "Sure that—"

"Hey Mad," a voice interrupted their conversation as Bo Dylans slid into place behind Maddie in line. "How's it going? Great game the other night, double-double and all…" he whistled in approval.

Maddie grinned and thanked him. As the line inched forward, the two continued to discuss the game and Cornelious watched in amusement as Eric's jaw set and his fists tightened.

Before Cornelious could think of something to say, Carly leaned in to whisper to Eric, "Don't worry. She is not into Bo Dylans and never will be."

Even though that fact was obvious, Cornelious felt his mood lighten a little, and saw the tension go out of Eric, as he grinned in response, "Thanks."

After each person had swiped their meal cards to pay, Eric and Bo went their own separate ways, and the trio met up with Pilot. He had managed to secure an end-of-the-table spot, in the center of the cafeteria for the four of them. Although it was a clutch location, the fact he had managed to procure four spots, in the overcrowded cafeteria, left the gang a little suspicious.

"How'd—" Carly began, and realized the people next to her slid a little further when she sat down as well.

Pilot smiled meekly, "I told them that my friends were arriving and have a serious case of gas today."

The foursome laughed, and their happiness was only interrupted by the arrival of a pretty red-head.

"Hey guys, Merry Christmas!" Alexis said, as she surveyed the group and laid her hand down on Cornelious' shoulder.

"Umm yeah, Merry Christmas," Pilot answered warily, knowing that if Maddie still didn't trust her, it would be wise if he did the same.

"Oh, Pilot, I wanted to say. Great presentation in Music. Your Google Slides were hilarious, and I have to agree with Carly that your tech skills are way underrated." As she faced Pilot, she made sure to swish her sequenced red and green holiday dress, captivating everyone's attention.

"Umm, thanks Alexis," Pilot glanced unsurely at Maddie, who shrugged, and dove into her delicious Brady's platter.

"And Maddie I heard you had a double last night—" Awesome."

Maddie was caught off guard at the compliment.

She wanted to reply, you mean double-double, but instead heard herself choke out, “Oh, uh thanks.”

“Anyway, I wanted to let you know I won’t be in town over break anymore—I’m going to Bali—and so my party is off. But I’ll make it up at a later date… and if any of you,” she turned to look Cornelious in the eyes, “want to chat, I’ll have my phone and full service.”

Knowing that she was clearly talking to him, Cornelious replied, “Oh, uh, good to know. Thanks.”

Alexis giggled and sashayed her way down the aisle, back to her table.

Maddie’s eyebrows squirmed upwards, “What’s that about?”

“What?” Cornelious asked, biting into his piece of heaven—the taco-pancake.

Maddie exhaled, and motioned to Alexis and her table, “Are you two… um… a two?” Maddie asked her best friend, feeling a rush of heat rise from the pit of her stomach to her face. She hoped it wasn’t showing.

Luckily, no one noticed. Carly and Pilot stayed quiet as they watched their friends’ awkward conversation.

“What? Me and Alexis?” Cornelious chuckled, but then considered the past few weeks and how often she had been at his side, whether inside or outside of school. Shaking his head no, he quickly answered, “No… not at all… it’s not like we’re dating. She just seems to like to talk to me and stuff.”

“Seems like she’s hoping for more of the stuff,” Maddie muttered, picturing her arch-enemy hanging out with her best friend.

Carly, as adept at sensing a blowout as geologists at

assessing when a volcano will blow, expertly turned the subject away from Alexis—who, although had been nicer to Pilot and Maddie lately, still had to be handled with suspicion—"I don't even know if there's going to be any party this break! It seems everyone is going away. And the winter formal is after Christmas break this year, which is weird but I guess they couldn't find a DJ in time, or something. And I just bought a brand-new dress too." Carly pouted and sadly pictured her shiny, new dress hanging in the back of her expansive closet, cold and lonely…

Cornelious responded with a half-smile, "Well, you know my dad is still planning a mega New Year's Eve party this year, instead of a Christmas Ball, so that's something to look forward too."

Carly shot up straight and beamed, "Yay!" Then she turned to her boyfriend, "You are not working it this year! You are my date."

Pilot shone brighter than Gotham's bat-light, "I wouldn't want it any other way."

10

As should be expected, the New Year's Eve party at the Gibbz's estate was thoroughly prepared to be a blowout. First-time mayor, Jeremiah Gibbz, wanted all Asbury citizens to feel welcome and decided that this year he would only hire out of town caterers and servers, for he wanted to extend an open invitation for all to attend. Nancy proposed they celebrate Cornelious' Sweet Sixteen at the party as well—since it would only be ten days after he turned sixteen. It was clear that Jeremiah wasn't too keen on having his son steal the show and was at a loss of how to reply to his beaming wife.

Luckily, Cornelious had already planned to spend his Sweet Sixteen at the Petrozza's, watching Christmas-themed horror movies while gorging on Mrs. Petrozza's homemade ice-cream cake. Thus, while Nancy and Jeremiah awkwardly sat across from each other, reflecting on how to persuade the other to his/her own cause, Cornelious slipped upstairs to his bookcase/bedroom door, and removed a faux hardback of 'Catch-22.' Inside, he removed a document that he had prepared five years ago—signed by both parents—stating that his birthdays belonged to him and only he could choose how to spend them. Neither parent was surprised, as he was taught at the tender age of four how to negotiate. Let's just say dinner/dessert time got interesting for a while there.

After scanning the document, Jeremiah let out a breath of relief, and Nancy frowned—until Cornelious pointed out that she could always help plan Carly's Sweet Sixteen this upcoming summer. Instantly cheering up, Nancy asked Cornelious if Carly would be opposed to attaching one-hundred-dollar bills to the invitations, as a way to stir up excitement. Cornelious realized how lucky he was to have dodged that bullet himself, but told his mom she'd have to ask Carly herself… and that she'd have to also supply the Benjamins.

Nancy laughed and said, "Of course, honey. We'll invite each kid in your class too." Most people would gawk at the idea of sending out close to three hundred, one-hundred-dollar bills, for something as trivial as an invitation. But to Nancy that amounted to less than her quarterly spa treatment, so was about as important to her as a hot date to Homecoming. Nice to have, but not necessary.

To be honest, the Gibbz's had a better turnout than expected. Those with young children or years-long traditions of celebration stayed home to celebrate their own way. However, many West-siders felt the attractive pull of being able to see the inside of the Gibbz estate and flocked to 2234 Red Oak Drive.

To best prepare for the celebrations, the front lawn of the Gibbz' estate was covered with tents and various carnival-like vendors, to best entertain the young ones. Balloons, cotton candy, and drinks were free of charge, as were the rides and games that each booth offered. Moving past the carnival-like atmosphere, the front doors of the mansion resembled welcoming arms thrown ajar for all to enter. Of course, most rooms were off-limits, and entrance to the grand staircase and upper levels were prohibited by use of a beautifully adorned (expensive, yet temporary) marble gate—only allowing access to the three Gibbz family members with ID cards. Even though Jeremiah was welcoming the public into his home, there were necessary limits in place—to keep a level of privacy intact for the photo-op-publicity-loving-family.

However, the downstairs provided enough room for people to hang out and celebrate the New Year. Jeremiah had a bar installed in both the dining room to the left of the entrance (having removed the family dining table), as well as across the hall in the den/living room. Naturally, the kitchen was the hub for the chefs, headed by none other than the venerable Chef Ski. But tonight, it had more of a hibachi feel as the chefs welcomed the guests to watch them cook and prepare the various food items they created. Throughout the entire house, musicians were spread out playing smooth jazz to welcome each visitor, as well as the New Year.

Exiting the kitchen, and the house, through the huge

glass sliding doors, one was transported into a Great Gatsby-like party. Bright white lights and chandeliers extended as far as the eye could see. These lights were strung from the back of the house, atop the large deck, all the way to the tree line at the back of the property. Most guests didn't even realize they had stepped outside, because the lighting, cleanliness, numerous tabletops and the ten-person band led many to believe they were still inside.

Just as important as decorating the estate, the Gibbzs themselves made sure they were primped and photo-ready. Of course, Jeremiah and Nancy were much more enthusiastic than their only son over appearances, and made sure to hand-pick his clothing. Luckily for Cornelious, he found he was rather comfy in the white polo shirt, with a golden splatter tastefully woven into the fabric, and a pair of dark black jeans with some white and black vans. Plus, his cousin Dane had arrived earlier that morning, and took both Nancy and Jeremiah's advice to heart, which helped take the focus off of him. Expensively dressed in a golden sport coat atop a plain black tee-shirt, Dane stepped out into the yard wearing one of a kind black and white Nike dress shoes (which Cornelious had politely declined the day before), and easily mingled with the best of the best, doing his Uncle proud.

Jeremiah, already imposing in stature, decided a purple three-piece suit showed off his best attributes. Nancy, ever the beauty queen, had three different outfits designated for various points in the night. She would begin by welcoming guests in a white power suit, with red heels and her grandmother's red rubies. After cocktail-hour, and before the buffet service began, she quickly changed into a floor length red dress, that royally flowed about her as she walked. And finally, right before midnight, Nancy chose a beautiful handmade black and gold maxi-dress that hugged her figure in all the right places, providing her with the regal appearance she sought after.

Feeling like a third wheel to Carly and Pilot, as well as pretty underdressed in her jeans, chucks, and long gray sweater, Maddie couldn't believe how quickly and totally the Gibbz had transformed their house.

"I feel like we've been transported in space or time," Maddie murmured to her friends.

Carly spun around in her long black skirt, as Pilot watched transfixed. "Or both," Carly decided, appraising her surroundings.

Looking over his beautiful girlfriend, Pilot once again felt grateful how this past year had turned out. He was even more hopeful for the coming year, and felt big things were ahead for himself and his friends. Pilot was even proud of how he nicely he was dressed, in a navy-blue long-sleeved dress shirt, and khaki pants—he had to give credit to Chanaki though. Since his mother had begun seeing his teacher, she had been happier than ever, and Chanaki had actually given him some pretty solid advice.

"Hi guys! You all look so wonderful! Maddie, I LOVE that sweater, and Pi, who would've thought you could look so handsome!... Isn't tonight just perfect?! I can't imagine all the planning and preparation Mr. and Mrs. Gibbz had to do!" Alexis, in a bright yellow knee-length dress, gushed to the trio and genuinely smiled.

Maddie thought the smile looked a little too similar to a crocodile, but just nodded along as Alexis and Carly conversed about their jewelry choices. Hannah, who was wearing a blue and gold long romper, struck up a conversation with Pilot about the New Year, and how she couldn't believe that people still believed in it. After all, she pointed out, there's nothing new about January, since she had learned about its existence in first grade.

At around seven, Jeremiah and Cornelious made their entrance into the backyard, as Nancy—who was greeting guests initially—quickly went upstairs for round one of her wardrobe changes.

While the Gibbz trio were making their rounds, Dane made his way over to Maddie, Pilot and Carly. Smirking, he ran his hand back through his curly hair, and said, "Last time I saw you guys, I made the mistake of leaving a treasure chest with you… you haven't happened to see it, have you?"

The three teens laughed and greeted Dane. After catching up, Dane was genuinely happy that Pilot and Carly were still an item, and that Maddie was still quite single. Even though most people, including himself, had dressed to the nines, he found himself unable to look away from the girl wearing jeans and chucks. Unfortunately, he wasn't able to get Maddie alone and couldn't spend too much time trying either, as he and Jeremiah had game-planned who Dane should spend time with tonight, in order to help boost his contacts for his future in office. After all, Dane considered as he left the trio to talk to the Henry's of the national Henry's Hardware chain, girls dig power, and he was surely on the path to a lifetime of it.

For the next half hour, Maddie, Pilot and Carly waited around and snacked on some delicious grub, as

Cornelious made his obligatory greetings. When he was finally able to break away, he grabbed a monstrous looking chocolate shake, and gulped it down in front of his friends.

"Before dinner?" Carly chided.

"I feel like I've been on stage on day," Cornelious replied. Maddie handed him a napkin, and he swiftly wiped away the chocolatey mustache from his upper lip.

"Well, you're the best show-dog we know," Maddie smiled, then added, "Other than Dane," gesturing to his cousin, who was vigorously shaking hands with Mrs. O'Neill, the second wealthiest person in town (and an original Parcels of Pecunia member to boot!).

Cornelious laughed and asked if they had run into anyone from school, as the crowd out here seemed more adult than teen.

"I actually think Jason was having some people over at the Luxurious Lady tonight," a sweet voice sang out from behind the group. "His dad told him it was fine and left him there completely unsupervised."

The last bit of news didn't surprise the gang, as T.J. Scott wasn't exactly the gold standard when it came to being a role model. Working hard? Sure. Parenting? Not so much.

"It's probably for the best," Cornelious stated. "I mean it's not like my parents would let them deviate from tonight's activities. They're probably having more fun."

"Being barbarians," Pilot considered, not wanting to admit they'd be having a better time with Jason Scott.

"More like regular teenagers," Carly looked at Pilot, who shrugged and answered, "I'd rather be with you guys."

Before anyone could answer, Jeremiah called

Cornelious over to meet someone, and Alexis decided it was a good time to go to the bathroom, leaving the trio alone to order some of their own milkshakes.

"Oh! I should probably grab us some more napkins first! Did you see how messy Cornelious was?" Carly realized in horror. After all of the effort she had spent preparing for tonight and her first New Year's kiss with Pilot, she was not going to look anything less than flawless.

Pilot and Maddie laughed, but Carly was determined and headed into the kitchen to grab a stash of napkins. Seeing there were only decorative ones set out, Carly headed into the back cabinet to where she knew the paper products were stored. Closing the cabinet, she froze when she overheard familiar snickering from around the corner.

"I mean, I wish you were here. Naturally, Cornelious looks sooo hot and Carly is well, you know Carly. But why she chooses to date that absolute nerd…"

Carly balled her fists in anger, as she realized she was overhearing Alexis talking on her phone to someone.

Alexis continued after a moment's pause, probably as the person on the other end of the line was speaking. "You would die! He's obviously trying so hard in his little sailor outfit, with that navy-blue long-sleeve and khaki pants!"

For the first time, Carly felt the need to strike Alexis. She knew she shouldn't be too surprised—after all Maddie had voiced this opinion for years. But Alexis was always cool to her, and they had been on the same squad for years. If she wasn't going to be friendly, at least there should be a shred of loyalty somewhere.

"And Madeline—HA! She's the opposite of a try-hard. At least I hope that her grandma sweater and secondhand jeans aren't an indication of her trying, because then that's just sad and I shouldn't be laughing… I guess," Alexis added as she burst out laughing.

Hearing all she needed, Carly took the high road, and strode away from the cabinet, towards her friends on the back deck. For better or worse, she was left to stew in her own anger for a few minutes, as Maddie and Pilot were at the front of the line ordering their shakes. Making their way to her, Carly's anger only increased as she realized that her friends may not be fashionably-savvy, but they were the best people she knew, and wouldn't change them for the world. For a second, she debated not telling them what she overheard. What good would that do? Other than hurt their feelings, and she knew how sensitive Pilot was.

Unfortunately, the decision was made for her when Pilot handed Carly her milkshake and frowned. "What's wrong, Car?"

Similar to a levy breaking after a Category Five hurricane, the conversation she had overheard came spilling out.

"I knew her recent nicey-nice attitude towards us was just an act!" Maddie proclaimed. Maddie was more happy than angry. Alexis had revealed her true colors and Carly was finally able to see Alexis for who she is.

"Why would she feel the need to act nice?" Carly questioned. "Why not just ignore you guys then?"

Pilot stared at Carly and answered the obvious, "For Cornelious. She's obsessed with him. She knows she'd have no shot with him if we all hated her… or at least, didn't want to be near her."

Carly knew Pilot was right, but was still visibly angry. "It doesn't give her a right to be so…so…so mean!"

Maddie shrugged, "It's just her personality."

"We need to tell Cornelious. Immediately." Carly's mouth had set in grim determination, and there was no changing her mind. The trio split up to find Cornelious and fill him in on the drama. As Carly said, we must save him from her clutches—and Maddie couldn't agree more.

Unfortunately, it was slow-going for the gang. Carly got caught talking to Nancy Gibbz for the next twenty minutes, and Pilot's task of scouring the backyard proved more difficult than he thought. To be honest, with all the bright lights and music playing, he got lost more than once.

Maddie was perusing the inside of the house, when she saw a swoosh of curly-red hair steer a white and gold shirt into the den. Imagining the lies Alexis was about to spew to her best friend, Maddie followed the pair into the den.

Turning the corner, Maddie slowed down as she saw there was no one else in the room, and it was a little too quiet. Holding her breath, Maddie peered into the corner of the den, where the newly set-up bar was currently deserted, and felt her heart drop. Grabbing his shirt, Alexis pulled Cornelious to her and pressed her lips firmly onto his. After two quick heartbeats, Maddie realized that Cornelious wasn't pulling away and actually seemed to enjoy the kiss!

Spinning on the heels of her Converses, she left the den and headed straight to the hidden bathroom across the hall and under the staircase. Shutting the door, Maddie leaned her back against the frame and rested her head against the oak wood. She couldn't believe it! Cornelious and Alexis! She knew they had gone to that dumb dance together last year, but she thought Cornelious had ditched Alexis for a reason. How could Cornelious possibly fall for that red-headed jerk?! The Cornelious she knew could never be so dumb, her Cornelious would've pushed away Alexis—nicely, though, he is a nice guy—and explain he wasn't into her. Maddie looked into the mirror and tried to voice the many thoughts and feelings bubbling inside of her. She was angry and shocked yes, but for some reason she felt… sad? Hurt? And why was she thinking of Neal as *her Cornelious*?

Maddie quickly turned on the faucet and splashed some cold water onto her face. She was more than just mad at her best friend, but didn't want to waste any more time thinking about it. Every time she replayed the kiss she just witnessed, she felt like vomiting. When she regained her composure, Maddie realized she couldn't tell Pilot or Carly what she saw. Maddie couldn't explain why, but it made her feel more than upset or angry, and she felt something big would change in telling them how she felt or if they saw her reaction. And that would be a mistake, she thought. So, Maddie resolved to keep it a secret. At least, for now.

11

With the New Year beginning, the gang was surprised to realize they were pretty much halfway through their school year. Although not much had changed, and their current investigation was slow-going, Cornelious felt there was a shift in the atmosphere of their group dynamic. For the past week, Cornelious felt that Maddie had been avoiding or at least evading him—for no reason! And having every class together didn't seem to be of any help to him in trying to determine what was on her mind. He would've just shaken it off as midterm stress—as midterms were coming up—but he knew Maddie wasn't one to stress over tests. Especially because she knew she'd ace them. However, even Carly's attitude had also changed. And she really wasn't one to worry over tests.

Twice this past week, the four of them had been walking to class, when out of nowhere Carly would clam up and grab Pilot's hand and walk away. The first couple of times Cornelious thought they wanted privacy before class. But then he realized that Maddie would also either speed up and head to class on her own or shrink away and almost disappear. Each time Cornelious was left baffled and would have questioned his friends for their behavior if Alexis and Hannah or Alexis and Jason hadn't popped up by his side. Clearly, he was missing something obvious. Frustratingly, he had no clue.

As a member of the cheer squad with Alexis, Carly discovered that Alexis and Cornelious had kissed and were "getting closer" (as Alexis eagerly told the team), the day after Maddie saw it herself. Not able to contain her newly gathered intel, Carly revealed her knowledge to Maddie and Pilot right away.

"Well, what should we do?" Pilot had asked at the time. The group was at a loss. They knew they wouldn't just give up their lifelong friendship with Cornelious. On the same token, none of them wanted to be around Alexis more than was necessary. Even Carly had started to mentally tally all of the times she had excused Alexis' obnoxious or just plain old rude ways, in favor of keeping the peace between her two worlds. Never again, Carly vowed. She was done with defending a bully. For pure and simple, that is what Alexis is.

The trio decided to see if there was any truth to the rumor of Cornelious and Alexis 'getting closer.' Honestly, the three of them couldn't see it—but, Alexis was making herself more visible in their daily lives. Whether it was walking with Cornelious in the halls, or sitting with them for the last few minutes of lunch each day, she was around. Unspoken between them, Carly, Pilot, and Maddie ultimately decided to wait and see if Cornelious truly wanted to date Alexis or if he was just being nice. Each of them prayed for the latter.

During the second week of January, Cornelious was sitting in first period wondering where Maddie could be—surely, she wouldn't skip school without telling him first. And especially not while in season, where missing a practice meant sitting out a game or forfeiting a starting position. Both options were such that Maddie would never consider skipping, Cornelious knew. With five minutes left in second period, Maddie entered the classroom, holding an unfamiliar pink slip in her hand, and a scowl on her face. Taking her seat in front of him, she began to pull out her notebook in an effort to copy whatever she could from the board.

Although Cornelious realized that seeing his best friend walk in provided him a great sense of relief (he hadn't been able to think of anything else all class), he also saw that she looked a little upset. Thinking, for some reason, that maybe it was his fault, Cornelious tapped her on the shoulder and whispered, "Are you okay?"

Maddie's shoulders slumped as she turned to face him, "Yeah. Eddie is on vacation this month and with Trent still not driving to school, the bus is my only option… And guess who is filling in for Eddie while he is in Cocomo?... Mrs. Shiffler."

Cornelious frowned, "Rodney's mom?"

"Yup. I guess she blames me for last year." Maddie

whispered.

Cornelious digested this information as the bell rang. The two got up to walk out of the door, when Cornelious felt a tap on his shoulder. He turned to face Alexis smiling sweetly at him, and realized she was asking him a question. With his mind was still on Maddie, he wasn't able to focus on whatever Alexis was saying and turned back to face his best friend. Realizing she was walking out of the door, he hurried to catch up to her (leaving an angry Alexis in his wake).

"Mads. What's up?" Although Cornelious meant in regards to her and Pilot and Carly's recent behavior, Maddie was still stuck on today's developments.

Maddie sighed and held out the pink slip. "I tried to explain to Coste what had happened, but he just replied with a detention slip and said, get this, '*maybe this detention will teach you not to meddle in other's personal affairs*."

****

Before walking into Mr. Chase's after school detention class, Maddie took a deep breath and reminded herself that a detention wasn't such a big deal. After all, she didn't plan on becoming a regular. And speaking of regulars, Maddie wasn't surprised to see JB and a handful of his loyal Pitbulls scattered throughout the small classroom. Maddie may have been the only girl there, but she was surprised to see a familiar face in the back right corner waving her over.

"Eric?"

Eric Henry smiled from his corner desk, and shrugged, "How's it going?"

Maddie laughed. Although JB turned to glare at her, it was nice to have a friend to pass the next hour with. Even if he looked more like an American Eagle model in a back to school ad than someone who should be sitting near a group of delinquents, as the Pitbulls were surrounding the happy-looking teen.

"What's so funny girly? And where's your boyfriend at—or did you trade up?" JB spat, literally causing her to back up as to avoid his phlem.

"Boyfriend?" Eric asked, sounding hurt.

Maddie rolled her eyes, and took a seat next to Eric. "Just ignore him. He means Cornelious, because he's never been able to talk to a member of the opposite sex and therefore, doesn't understand the word friends."

Eric visibly lightened and smiled back at JB.

JB's eyes turned to slits. "I talk to girls. I'm talking to you now."

"I'd say that's more of threatening than engaging in a good conversation," Maddie pointed out, as she began pulling out various sheets of homework and to-do lists from her purple bookbag.

Eric laughed, and JB spun back around determined to ignore the two goody-two shoes who were invading his domain (as he viewed after school detention). In fact, unbeknownst to Maddie and her friends, after-school detention was often where JB and his gang passed along information and tidied up business deals—as he liked to think.

So, for the next forty-five minutes, JB and his Pitbulls exchanged notes and whispers, while Maddie and Eric finished some homework and talked about random subjects such as sports, or recent adventures the both had undergone. For the latter, Maddie described her winter break babysitting trials with her younger twin siblings and their friends, Kimi Davies (Milton's younger sister, who was a frequent at twin-events), and the Sobrinski children (a batch of kids ranging in age from two to seven), while Eric detailed the faraway places he had visited. It was nice and easy conversation, and Eric wasn't trying to show off, as Maddie used to think, but rather tell her of his own experiences there. He even joked it would be fun if she joined him on a family vacation one time. At least Maddie thought he was joking…

With close to ten minutes left, the generally calm atmosphere of the Mr. Chase's small detention room was upended. The bald-headed-Bluetoothed fury of Principal Coste burst into the room. Anyone would've sworn before a judge that his face was redder than fresh lava flowing from a volcano and that actual steam poured out of his ears.

"YOU!" his single finger pointed to JB with such outrage, that it seemed JB was being condemned to the guillotine before their eyes.

"Wh—what? Sir." JB stammered, not usually intimidated by Coste but sensing open hostility.

"A half hour ago, I parked my car in the lot and now I return to see the tires have been slashed!"

It took JB a good minute to realize the indication of Coste's accusing finger. "But…I didn't do it!"

Coste didn't want to hear any excuses, and started spewing off threats of expulsion and mandatory janitorial services with Janitor Cutro (making even Maddie shudder).

Maddie, never one to stand by as a bully has his

way, stood up and defended her foe. "Mr. Coste, I'm sorry but it's impossible for JB to have slashed your tires. He was in detention with all of us the whole time and never even left the room to use the bathroom. In fact, none of us have left the room."

Coste lowered his finger and slid his eyes from JB to Maddie, then back to JB.

Calmly, Mr. Chase (not wanting any ire to spill over onto him), sat up from his corner desk, and gently told his boss, "Ms. Petrozza is correct… sir. No one has been in, or out, since detention officially began."

"That may be true." Pausing to consider, "I don't know what's going on in here, but just know I have my eyes on you. Both." The vengeful Principal glared at the two teens, before nodding over to Mr. Chase. Exiting the room, Coste stormed out with great wrath, causing the papers taped outside the door to flutter down the hallway, leaving chaos in the principal's path.

Mr. Chase, happy to be safe from Coste's rage, announced detention time was up and they should all head home. No one dared to point out that there was still a half hour left on the clock, but this way they could avoid Janitor Cutro's bickering over having to resweep the hall.

Walking out the door, JB faced Maddie and said, "Don't think this means I'm thankful or I owe you nothin'."

Maddie read in his face how grateful he was and saw he was still a little shaken up. For everyone knows, Coste isn't one to abide by school or even legal procedures and would lie before a jury and deny any punishment he imposed that might be frowned upon by law. Maddie brushed past JB, with Eric following suite, and without looking back replied, “I wouldn’t think of it.”

As they neared the exit, Maddie saw Carly standing outside waiting for her. She appeared to be silently going over a new cheer and was throwing her arms out, deftly practicing the moves. Either that or she joined Asbury’s (creepy) mime club without informing her friends.

Eric and Maddie passed through the glass doors and walked down the three cement stairs, down to the sidewalk. Eric nodded Carly, but wasn’t certain she saw him through her mental preparations. Maddie stopped when they reached her friend, while Eric saluted a goodbye to Maddie, and continued on down the sidewalk.

Maddie, realizing she never asked, jokingly called out, “Hey! I never asked, what were you in for?”

Eric looked stunned, and cocked his head sideways. “Me? I didn’t have detention. I just knew you did.” He smirked, put his hands in his sweatshirt and walked away down the block.

“And what, exactly, was that about?” Carly’s smile turned up in intrigue and her mind was spinning possibilities.

Before Maddie could even think of a reply, the girls were interrupted by Right Said Fred singing out ‘I’m Too Sexy,’ from Carly’s bag.

“Oh! That’s Pilot!” Carly said as she dug through her bag to claim her cell.

Maddie groaned and smacked her hand to her forehead, “Your ringtone for Pilot is the ‘I’m Too Sexy’ song?”

Carly glared at her friend, and listened to her

excited boyfriend ramble on the other end. “Okay,” she said, “Got it.”

Carly slid her phone back into her bag and relayed the news to Maddie. “There’s been another case of identity theft at the Asbury Bank.”

12

Under regular circumstances, Maddie's mind would've been reeling over what Eric Henry had just admitted. He had spent his afternoon in detention with her, just to hang out? Surely, there were other ways of getting her attention, although with school, sports, and their semi-active investigation, it seemed her time was in short supply. Nevertheless, Maddie's thoughts steered clear of Eric and were zoned in on the latest news from Pilot.

"Quick! There's the trolley!" Maddie grabbed Carly's wrist and sprinted to the trolley, as it was stopped on the corner at the traffic light. Happily surprised, Maddie saw her two teammates standing towards the back. "Come on, let's see what I missed at practice."

Carly looked where Maddie was heading and

decided to follow her friend. Even though she wasn't one to talk sports, the fact that the two girls in the back were Nya Carr and Ana Carmen, made Carly just as eager to see them as Maddie. Perhaps the funniest person in their grade, Nya was always quick with a joke or a hilarious impression, when needed the most. She also was an assassin with a basketball, and was already deciding between two top Division one colleges in the country to attend. Ana, although a year younger and only a freshman, was Nya's best friend. Maddie had frequently mentioned that her skills as a point guard was the last missing piece that they needed to win the States—and apparently the entire school agreed. What made Carly like the girl even more was that she had twice declined an offer from Jason to go on a date. Plus, as a bilingual speaker she had the coolest accent and was apt to bring in homemade Puerto Rican dishes to lunch—which she also generously shared with any who asked, much to Carly and Pilot's delight (as she sat behind them in the cafeteria).

For the short journey to the Owens', Nya reenacted various times in practice where Willy had each girl busting up—whether intentional or not—and even Carly felt as if she was there. Sensing Maddie was saddened to have missed a practice Ana quickly pointed out, "but don't worry Willy wasn't upset that you missed… he says he understands as he knows Mrs. Shiffler *intimately*."

Nya smirked, "Yeah, apparently they used to date when they went to Asbury High 'back in the day,'" ending with a perfect imitation of their beloved coach.

Laughing again, the foursome quickly moved their conversation from basketball to boys… in which Maddie and Carly both clammed up when Nya brought up Alexis and Cornelious. Luckily, the trolley stopped in front of Henry's Hardware—where Mr. Carmen worked—before either girl had to tackle that drama.

When the two girls finally arrived at Pilot's, Ms. Owens threw open the door and beamed at each of them. She had always loved them both as daughters, but ever since discovering that Pilot and Carly were dating, they had felt her love deepen even further.

"Girls! How have you been? Anything new on the horizon?" Ms. Owens inquired, stepping aside to allow the girls entry.

Maddie shrugged noncommittally, knowing Carly would answer for the both of them. "Not really. Maddie's been close to averaging a double-double in points and rebounds this season, and their freshmen point guard Ana has been killing it. They actually only have one loss and are still undefeated in their conference."

Jenna Owens absolutely shined. She had seen Maddie commit countless hours to athletic endeavors her whole life, and was proud her hard work was paying off.

Maddie blushed, "It helps to be surrounded by really good teammates."

"CARLY?! MADDIE?! IS THAT YOU?! COME ON UP!" Pilot's voiced boomed from upstairs.

"Well, I guess that's our cue," Maddie smiled, and the two raced up the stairs.

Cornelious held the door open for the two of them, and quickly shut it after they entered. Carly sat down to Pilot's right, after kissing him quickly on the cheek. Though second-nature on her part, Pilot found the warm sensation of blood still raced to his cheeks during such moments.

Noticing his blush, Maddie and Cornelious grinned at each other and took their seats on the floor in front of Pilot's bed, facing the downward sliding projector.

"How was detention?" Cornelious asked cautiously, as if not sure if it was an okay topic to breach.

Maddie smiled, "It was fine actually. I ended up hanging with Eric the whole time—and Coste exploded on JB for no reason too. It would've been fun, if JB wasn't so shaken up…I ended up standing up for the kid." Recalling the scene, Maddie shook her head good-naturedly.

"Eric Henry had detention? He's even less likely to get detention than you," Cornelious pointed out, skipping over the fact that Maddie had stood up for JB. For some reason, he felt there was something wrong with Eric going to detention.

"Yeah, well, apparently he didn't even have detention." Maddie held out her hands, showing that she was equally as confused as he.

Befuddled by this revelation, Cornelious was about to question what Maddie meant, when Pilot cleared his throat and began his report.

"Yet again, another person has gone to the Asbury Police and reported a large sum of money withdrawn aka STOLEN from their account, early this morning. The police have even brought in online identity theft professionals, because it is their belief that the crook or crooks are doing this all online." Pilot paused for dramatic effect, as he brought up some incomprehensible matrix type numbers and JavaScript text across the screen. "However, after extensive research on my part, I think it is IMPOSSIBLE that someone is committing these crimes online. There is no trace of any activity—and I'm 100% sure of my findings," Pilot declared, satisfied with his presentation.

"So, what does that mean?" Carly asked.

It seems all four were thinking the same thing: If the thefts weren't happening online, then how come the bank security didn't step in, or police weren't able to look up footage and arrest whoever they saw taking the money from the account at the time of the reported heist?

"It means that the theft must be happening at the bank, in person," Pilot still sounded hesitant.

"You look hesitant, Pi," Cornelious remarked on the obvious.

"Well, that's because I have all footage from every camera at the bank and there seems to be nothing out of the ordinary."

"So…the money is what? Being taken by Houdini?" Maddie half-joked.

Clicking off the screen, Pilot faced his friends. "At this point, that seems the most logical."

"Well, what are we supposed to do? Stake out the bank at all hours?" Carly asked exasperated. Usually the least likely to jump into investigations, this one was greatly piquing her interest. How could so much money go missing?

Maddie shook her head, "We can't even do that. There's no clear pattern and it seems as if the crooks are taking this money on a whim."

"What about the bank tellers? Isn't it suspicious

they're just reportedly handing over money?" Carly inquired.

Pilot nodded, "It seems there are two tellers, during any given shift, and they rotate on a three-shift schedule, so that make six possible suspects."

"Sounds like the title of one of the books I read in book club last year," Maddie murmured.

Undaunted Pilot continued, "And apparently, they've all been cleared of any wrongdoing. The ones who were working during the thefts claim they just run the withdrawals slips and paperwork handed to them and verified via FDIC security checks… But, interestingly enough, one of the tellers has been on shift during both thefts."

"What? That seems like big news! Who?" Carly spouted off quicker than

"Asbury High's very own computer teacher's—"

"Mrs. Dull?!" Maddie asked incredulously.

"No! Not her, you didn't let me finish…" Pilot took a deep breath and continued, "her husband, Brett Dull."

Cornelious considered this information and shook his head, "All because he's married to a high school computer teacher, doesn't mean he's as good with computers as she is… look at you and Carly. No offense."

"None taken. I agree with Cornelious, we can't jump to conclusions. Especially if Asbury Police cleared him already."

Maddie snorted. "Yeah, because they're the golden standard of police competency."

Carly ignored her friend. "I mean, we can add him to our nonexistent suspect list, but should keep an open mind."

Pilot, not one to be deterred, stood up and faced his friends. "I just remembered something important though… Brett Dull is Mr. Rhodes' brother in law."

"And?" Carly patiently asked.

"And," Pilot smiled knowingly, "that means he is part-owner to Rhodes Electronics, and has free access to the best technology on the market."

******

The week following the latest case of 'Missing Money', as every Asburyan was calling it, seemed to drag by. Coste was still stewing from his tires being slashed, and was handing out pink slips like it was Halloween. Pilot even invented a quick app called Circumventing Coste, where users (students and teachers alike) would tap in his whereabouts when he was spotted storming about the hallways. Although Pilot didn't charge any money for this app— and really started it as a joke—he found his popularity stock went way up. Not that he even cared. In fact, after obtaining such notoriety he admitted to his friends that he wished they kept the app between them. Sensing his unease, Carly reassured her boyfriend that teenagers have short memories and his fifteen minutes of fame would blow over.

Standing around Carly's locker after school, Pilot leaned against the side of her neighbor's locker and complained, "But what if this is just the beginning and I lose my…my…my…"

"Nerdiness?" Maddie laughed.

Pilot scowled, "I was thinking more of my sense of secrecy."

Cornelious, Maddie, and Carly laughed, and pretty soon Pilot was joining in, finding it impossible not to when surrounded by such whole-hearted mirth.

Carly shut her locker and was going to reassure Pilot, yet again, that all was well, when she felt a tap on her shoulder and spun to her left in reply.

"Oh, hi Anthony." Carly smiled, shutting her locker and facing the senior.

Anthony shuffled his feet a little and cleared his throat. "I was…um, uh… just wondering if you had any plans this weekend? I have off from work Saturday night and would love to take you out to dinner."

The gang was awkwardly stunned. Even those who hadn't known Pilot's name before this week had known Carly Cosentino was seriously dating a red-headed kid in her grade and was off limits. Much to the chagrin of many.

Before Pilot could erupt and cause a scene, Carly quickly answered, "Oh, Anthony I'm sorry. But Pilot is my boyfriend and that's not going to change anytime soon." Carly slipped her arm into Pilot's, and continued, "Thank you though, and I am sorry."

Clearly embarrassed, Anthony Dylans murmured an apology and sped on his heels down the hallway, and out the doors.

"Well, that was awkward," a familiar voice drawled out from behind the shocked group.

"Yeah, you can say that again," Maddie muttered, turning to see Alexis and her friends standing in full cheer gear (even though practice was cancelled), behind the gang.

"Well, that was awkward," Hannah Heston repeated, due to Maddie's request.

Maddie smiled at Hannah's innocence, before frowning at how keenly Alexis was staring into Cornelious' eyes. Yet again, the unfamiliar feeling of anger and nausea washed over Maddie, and her mind raced for an excuse to head outside.

Luckily, Alexis got right to the point. "Speaking of Saturday night, the winter formal is happening that night, and since I know you're not going, I figured it might be fun if we went together." Alexis sidled up to Cornelious and actually tossed her hair over her right shoulder.

Cornelious took a half a step back, and looked sincerely sorry. "I'm sorry Alexis, I actually have plans for Saturday night already." Seeing how dejected she looked, Cornelious quickly added, "But maybe another time."

That seemed to perk Alexis right up, as she grinned and replied, "I'll hold you to that, mister."

Oblivious to Cornelious, Carly, Pilot and Maddie inwardly groaned.

13

After adding nothing to their newest development in regards to their latest case, Maddie and Cornelious were happy they had more pressing matters on their mind. Although both the boys' and girls' teams were a shoe-in for playoffs, the boys conference race was much closer than that of the undefeated Asbury girls. In fact, Maddie's team could lose their next three conference game (which they intended not to do), and still win the conference title. The boys were neck and neck with Mainland—each suffering only one loss—and neither team wanted to forfeit the title.

Therefore, the first weekend game in February was not only held in Mainland during a snowstorm, but happened to be a double header.

As with most double headers, it was ladies first. For

the first quarter, Mainland proved a worthy adversary. It seemed the two teams were meeting shot for shot. It was 12-12, after eight minutes of play, and no one was smiling on the Asbury side.

At Ana's insistence, Asbury not only pressed full court but started employing more pump fakes. From her own personal scouting, Ana knew Mainland would jump at anything and, more often than not, foul. It seemed she knew her stuff, for Maddie tallied two quick steals in the first minute and Mainland's cheers died down faster than a politician's failed promise. At halftime, Asbury had jumped to a twenty-point lead, and would go on to win by thirty, with the starters sitting out the entire fourth quarter.

When the game ended and Willy finished his post-game speech, the girls quickly changed into their travel sweat-suits and headed to the bleachers to replace the boys' team, who had been cheering them on during their play.

When the whistle blew signaling that warm-ups were over and the game was about to begin, Cornelious jogged over to the sidelines and stepped on the bench, reaching over to high-five Maddie and tell her how great she played.

Maddie could tell Cornelious was nervous, but knew he would get into his groove in a matter of seconds. She wished him good luck and smiled at his nervous smile as he turned to face his coach in the huddle.

Even though the girls' game was entertaining, due to the undeniable skill of Asbury's players, the boys' game was a different story. From the jump, there was drama. As players from both teams dove after the ball, the Mainlander proved victorious and the Asburyan had to leave the court to quickly address his bloody nose.

After two quarters of hard-hitting action, Asbury found themselves up by a single point. Cornelious had risen to the top again, scoring twenty of Asbury's twenty-five points. He just could not, or would not, miss.

Baruff's halftime speech was meant to be inspiring, but he was yelling so much and creating so many nonsense words, that Cornelious and his teammates had to look down in order to stifle their laughter or hide their grins.

Mainland's halftime speech must've been taken more seriously, for they came out raging. Unfortunately, their rage resulted in more fouls than points scored. One defender appeared to tackle Cornelious as he went up for a reverse-layup, ending in a technical foul. Maddie's breath caught in her throat as it looked like Cornelious landed hard—but he sprang up and, smiling his goofy grin, headed to the stripe and sunk two shots. After that, it seemed Mainland lost their spirit and Asbury went on to win by five.

******

That night, dinner at Maddie's house was all about recounting the highlights of both games. Daniel and Shannon wouldn't budge from Cornelious' lap, leaving him to create original ways to eat his burger.

Hearing how dirty the boys' team played, and that his sister scored a team high twenty-eight points, Trent was pissed he had missed the games. But Mia had surprised him by cooking a special dinner at her house, and he was surprised to find she had become as talented a cook as she was a bad driver. He even found himself urging her to apply to culinary school, to which she just smiled and shook her head.

“Anyway, Cornelious, are you sure that last foul didn’t hurt you at all? I heard myself start praying before I even realized what I was saying,” Mrs. Petrozza worriedly asked.

Cornelious assured everyone he was fine, he had earned a couple of bruises, but no lasting injury. However, he was (as usual), touched at the genuine concern for his well-being that Maddie’s family had for him and was grateful he had the world’s best friend.

“Do you need to call your parents and tell them about the game, sweetie?” Mrs. Petrozza asked, depositing homemade dirt pudding onto the table.

Cornelious and Maddie’s eyes widened as they beheld Mrs. Petrozza’s famous dessert. Maddie had to remind Cornelious to answer her mom, in which he quickly responded, “I’m sure they’re very busy right now, and probably checked the box scores already.”

Maddie couldn’t imagine her parents not wanting to know every play-by-play of her games, but knew Jeremiah and Nancy were totally immersed in their Governorship Getaway in Stenton Township, and most likely forgot Cornelious had played today.

When any and all evidence of the dirt pudding was removed, Cornelious and Maddie made their way to Maddie’s bedroom and plopped down side by side on the bed.

“I heard there’s a new horror-comedy on Netflix,” Cornelious stated.

“I only like horror-comedies if M. Night Shyamalan made them.”

Cornelious laughed and they decided on a random murder-mystery that proved too boring to even pretend to follow.

"Holy cow," Cornelious muttered.

"What?"

"That red-headed heiress looks like Alexis Johnson."

Maddie glanced at Cornelious, unable to read his expression, and responded, "Kind of… I heard the two of you are pretty much dating."

Cornelious looked surprised and faced Maddie, "Dating? I wouldn't say that." He laughed and leaned back against the headboard. "No way."

Maddie waited for him to continue, yet somehow dreaded his response.

"She has technically asked me out, and texts me a few times a week. I mean, she seems like she's changed and matured—"

"Matured?" Maddie questioned; eyebrows raised.

"I mean, she doesn't seem as snobby as you've always said."

Maddie shook her head, "That's because she doesn't act that way in front of you."

Cornelious shrugged, "Maybe… she seems nice, and keeps mentioning that we have so much in common and should get to know each other better." Cornelious glanced sideways at Maddie's expressionless face. He frowned. "What?"

"Nothing. It's just… if she asked you out, maybe you should've gone then."

Cornelious considered it for a second before

answering, "Well, you and me already had plans for tonight."

It was Maddie's turn to laugh, "Neal, we're together every week and weekend. If you wanted to hang out with Alexis I would've understood." Hoping nothing betrayed her true thoughts (which she was still sorting out), Maddie felt her heart pound hard against her chest. She forcibly pushed away her thoughts of anger, and possible growing jealousy. She didn't care if Neal dated Alexis, it's not like they'd get married! Maddie inwardly gagged, just thinking about that only made her feel worse.

"I don't cancel plans I already made. That's one of the few things that my dad instilled in me that actually makes sense."

Maddie laughed at the joke, and they settled into a comfortable silence, both trying to get into the murder mystery but actively lost in their thoughts.

Time passed, but Cornelious couldn't get out of his own head. Maddie had a point, he told himself. He could've easily taken Alexis out and then crashed here at the Petrozza's. And he really did think Alexis had changed for the better. But, he questioned himself, why did he opt out? He further realized that given the choice between hanging with Maddie or going on a date (at least with Alexis), he would choose hanging with Maddie every time, hands down. Stealing another glance at his best friend, he wondered just what that meant.

14

The next morning, the Petrozza table was still buzzing with excitement over the double-header from the night before. Beating Mainland always gave Asburyans—East and West side alike—a natural high. This particular morning, there was extra fervor as the feature article in the local paper included an interview with a Mainland Senior on the team, who claimed the refs were against them the whole game.

After reading the article aloud, Mr. Petrozza folded the paper down and glanced about his angered audience. Even Sophia, who was busy flipping and distributing her famous coconut chocolate chip pancakes, burrowed her brows in ire.

Cornelious let out a deep breath and whistled low, "We'll just see how playoffs go then."

Maddie intoned that Mainland had just provided them with even more fuel for their fire. She could only imagine the backlash players like Jason or Nya would inflict on their next meeting with the Mustangs. The thought made her smile.

Daniel and Shannon's heads snapped to attention. "Fire?" they wondered together, eyes gleaming with the question.

Alec laughed, "Oh no!" and tried, fruitlessly, to grab the bottle of hot sauce away from his twin siblings' clutches. Unfortunately, the younger two were quicker, and Daniel was unscrewing the lid before Mrs. Petrozza even realized that they had decided to add their beloved red sauce to the entire stack of pancakes!

"Seriously, guys!" Sophia shrieked, welding the spatula like a weapon.

"I'm glad, I ate my five already," Trent murmured, pushing his chair back and bringing his plate to the sink.

Maddie and Cornelious shared a glance and also considered themselves lucky. Sophia's pancakes were no joke. In fact, Cornelious often remarked that she should try to get a job with Brandan and Dennis in the near future. Although only in fifth grade, Sophia had been gifted in the culinary arts. A gift that was becoming more and more delicious each day.

Of course, Sophia only blushed and turned back to her cooking in response to Cornelious' compliments. Sensing a fight was about to ensue, Mr. Petrozza asked if anyone could head to the auto shop and meet La.

Maddie volunteered herself and Neal, grabbing her best friend away from the table and out of the door, before

Mrs. Petrozza could start in on the twins—as they would (predictably) begin a tornado of destruction in the kitchen.

"That's why I love it here," Cornelious stated as the pair headed down the sidewalk to the Petrozza Auto Shop.

"Because they're crazy?" Maddie inquired.

Cornelious laughed, "Because you have a REAL family…and I never know what to expect."

Maddie grinned and pointed to her family's business. "Like La standing on top of an old school bus, surveying the auto shop lot with binoculars?"

Cornelious followed his friend's extended finger to see her famously outrageous grandmother actually standing on top of an old school bus, as if she was a lookout at sea. "And don't forget to add, in her curlers."

The two laughed and made their way to La. Staring up at her, and dodging a few lose rainbow-colored curlers, Maddie broke the silence.

"See any treasure up there?"

La turned her binoculars to the duo. "From what I hear, treasure is more up your alley." She winked conspiratorially, and leapt down to the hood of the bus. Swinging her zebra-jeans over the edge, La gracefully landed on her two feet and extended her arms to embrace the two teens.

"What exactly have you been up to La?" Cornelious asked innocently.

"Oh, I may be a jet-setting globe-trotting granny," she let go of the hug and put her hands on her hips, "but I have my informants all over. And let's just say I've stacked up quite a few favors from the Parcels of Pecunia over the years. But I won't waste time on that—this is all about the two of you."

Maddie smiled at her legendary grandmother and clarified, "Well, I won't confirm or deny any treasure officially… but it would seem that any type of endeavor would involve our whole gang."

La nodded knowingly, "I should've known Pilot and Ms. Cosentino would be crucial to any of the two of your doings," she paused to cackle, "or undoings."

Cornelious agreed, "You can't go to battle without all of your troops."

"Very wise, Mr. Gibbz." La snapped her fingers and stood alert. "Speaking of battle, I am enlisting you two to help me find an old, yet still bright purple box—hidden in a '76 Camaro."

"Should we even ask?" Maddie beamed, ready for yet another treasure hunt.

"You may think it unwise, but I'm very weary of banks. Especially big banks, and especially after learning of Asbury's recent banking… disappearances."

Maddie and Cornelious looked at each other.

"So, years ago, when I was about your ages actually, I vowed to stash money and goods all over the world in various places."

"That's insane La-La," Maddie warned.

"You sound like your dad," she grumbled. "And just about every other sane citizen." La laughed and turned her binoculars back to her eyes. "But it's worked for me for this long."

Before either of them could argue, La added "I do keep most of my finances and precious items locked up in numerous PO Boxes though. I don't like the idea of a mailbox where a nosy mailman—or woman—could shuffle through my mail or unknowingly read some classified information."

Cornelious and Maddie saw she wasn't kidding, and left it at that. Everyone's entitled to their own opinions and ways, as long as their ways don't hurt others. And truly, no one was any worse off for La's strange ways. In fact, she was in her seventies and thriving!

After a forty-five-minute search, Cornelious remembered Trent mentioning moving a '76 Camaro to the back of the shop, as a customer was interested in obtaining some parts.

Lo and behold, the Camaro was safely snuggled under a bright blue tarp, which La tore away voraciously.

"AHA!" A victorious cry pierced the crisp mid-morning winter air, as La reemerged with a bright purple box. It was only the size of an iPhone case, and Cornelious and Maddie were surprised to see La withdraw a silver chain necklace, holding a single, silver key. Slowly, and with great care, the duo watched as La slipped the necklace over her head and around her neck. Hiding it under her unique straw and feather scarf, she put one finger to her mouth in the universal sign of silence, and asked for discrepancy.

The duo nodded in assent, and the three of them headed back to the Petrozza household. Each hoping there were still pancakes left—untouched by the twins.

15

Even though the Mainlander's comments in the local paper caused quite a stir in school that Monday, the rest of the week passed amicably enough. Both the boys' and girls' teams won both of their games, and were already thinking of who they would face in the playoffs next week.

Peetie, as President of the Student Council, had even gotten Coste to agree to a Pep Rally preceding the playoff games. With her recent Model UN summer camp exposure, she had notebooks filled with school improvement ideas, including how to boost Aces pride. Her current campaign proved successful too, as she lured seniors into applying for small, underrated scholarships for college, by promising that for every two scholarship applications filled out the applier would receive a free movie ticket to the Moorlyn Cinema. Mrs. Moorlyn (owner of the cinema, whose husband worked at Asbury High), readily agreed to this as she knew she would make sales in candy, popcorn, and other various concessions. Plus, as the only theater in town she was always busy.

While Pilot was excited for his friends' successes, he was most excited for his Friday night Valentine's date with Carly. After a month of waiting, and an even longer time spent hacking into the restaurant's database, Pilot had managed to procure reservations for himself and Carly at Asbury's premier restaurant: Deborah's.

Thus, at precisely six-thirty, Pilot (or rather Mr Chanaki), picked up Carly from her house and drove to Deborah's. Pilot was happy to discover he liked Mr. Chanaki more and more with each passing day. He was also very thankful that his mom was dating an 'actual good guy.' He employed the phrase 'actual good guy' to describe Chanaki because it was a phrase he often heard the women in his life—Mrs. Petrozza, Mrs. Cosentino, his mom and even Carly—use. Especially when they were discussing how difficult a task it seemed to become to one (Pilot secretly hoped Mrs. Cosentino viewed him as one). Therefore, when Pilot told his mom and Mr. Chanaki of his dinner date plans to pick up Carly and head to the restaurant via bikes, Mr. Chanaki jumped right in and offered to chauffeur. He even promised, without Pilot's prompting, not to say a word. Although, once Carly jumped in the back seat with Pilot all three found themselves engaged in easy conversation.

At the restaurant, Pilot made sure to splurge on sparkling cider and hor de' oeuvres. He knew Carly wasn't necessarily impressed by fancy things, but he himself enjoyed a change every once in a while, and considered a fancy date to be a nice change of pace. Sitting under a grand chandelier, with at least five-hundred crystalized lightbulbs, it was easy to imagine the pair were on an overseas adventure, rather than dining luxuriously between the Krzyk Family Dental/Doctor offices and the Jennie Grace Salon.

During their entrée course, the conversation (inevitably) led to their friends and high school drama. Pilot revealed to Carly that Cornelious had confided in him that Alexis had caught him by his locker yesterday and boldly asked him out on an actual date. Pilot made sure to stress the word 'actual,' as he figured it was a popular buzz-word among girls.

Apparently, he was right, for Carly's eyes widened.

"What Did He Say?" Carly made sure to slowly draw out each word in the sentence.

Pilot swallowed a forkful of garlic mashed potatoes. "He said it was very awkward because they had been texting a lot lately and pretty much, as he said Alexis phrased it—getting to know each other better. Then he even more awkwardly told me how he and Alexis kissed on New Year's."

Carly swatted her hand away, as if to show the insignificance of that last part. "Well, we knew that."

"Yes, but he didn't know we knew that," Pilot countered. "And he revealed it to me as, 'she pulled me in the den and kissed me'.

"True... Don't leave me hanging here Pi."

Pilot put his hands up in defense, "Okay, okay.

Turns out, Cornelious turned her down and basically said he didn't want a girlfriend and honestly couldn't see himself dating anyone."

"Interesting," Carly grinned. Sipping her cider, she added, "Hopefully this means Alexis won't waste her time being so fake anymore."

Pilot was about to snort, *Fat chance*, but a shrill laugh coming from the table next to them grabbed both of their attention.

The laughter originated from a beautiful middle-aged amber-haired woman sporting a short bob. She was holding up a shiny necklace with one hand and sloshing a glass of red wine in the other.

"It's gorgeous," she gushed.

Pilot was shocked to realize that sitting across from this well-off bombshell was Post Officer Samuels. He didn't know how such a chill, down to earth guy would take someone out to such a fancy restaurant. But then again, he was here too.

"I can't believe those two are here together," Carly whispered, leaning in to Pilot.

"Me neither. I've never seen him wearing anything other than his Post Office getup! I mean, even at the Halloween ball…" Pilot trailed off looking at Carly's confused face.

"I meant, that's Margaret Steel. She's only into a certain type of guy, from a certain type of class. Basically, she's a jerk! Even if Mr. Samuels could afford to date her, she would never say yes! All based solely on his job and which side of Asbury he lives in," Carly explained, in a hushed voice.

Pilot nodded and just shrugged it off. With Carly as a girlfriend, he felt he was always learning something new about someone in Asbury, whether he wanted to or not.

"I also thought she was currently going after that Fireman who came to school on your birthday," Carly confided, as she reached across the table to stick a fork into Deborah's famous Haystack Double-Brownie, meant to share between two (although Cornelious and Maddie agreed that was debatable).

"You mean on Fire Awareness Day?" Pilot rolled his eyes at the memory. For as long as he could recall, Asbury schools had always held assemblies of some sort on his birthday. Not that he usually minded, it meant less work on his special day. But having a bunch of good-looking firemen give a talk to your school, after you managed to sit next to your girlfriend (who could barely contain her drool), wasn't exactly a highlight.

Carly smiled, "I thought it was an assembly on male models." She quickly added, "Joking," when Pilot's face fell. "Jeff McKinley and Jack Lombardi have nothing on you."

Another shrill bout of laughter exploded from Post Officer Samuels table, as Pilot and Carly watched him clasp the necklace around Margaret's neck. Carly's eyes widened, as she spun around and closed her hand around Pilot's. "I just remembered something from earlier this year!"

"Does it have to do with them?" Pilot asked, indicating the loud, albeit happy couple.

"No! Earlier this year, we were all pumped when Mrs. Dull let us play computer games all class…do you remember why?"

"Uh, because we got to play games, rather than learn an extremely elementary lesson on how to generate a high-traffic web—"

"Pilot Monet Owens! I was NOT asking why we were happy…I was asking why Mrs. Dull was so happy and carefree."

"Ohhhh…. I don't know then."

As their waiter dropped off a dessert menu, and left them time to read it over, Carly smiled. "Because," she leaned in, lowering her voice further, "her husband, Mr. Brett Dull had bought her a Swarovski diamond necklace, that she couldn't stop gushing over."

Pilot's eyes grew even wider than Carly's, if possible. "Oh man! That's proof there! We gotta get back to the gang."

"I know! But Cornelious is out of town tonight with his parents at some dinner, and I already made plans to sleep at Maddie's. I'll fill her in when I get there, and you can text or call Cornelious when we get back, too. We're having a girl's night and I don't want to spend the whole night discussing the case… in fact, I may just leave it out until the morning," Carly decided.

After their stomach had expanded to their capacity, and the two had taken a little boardwalk stroll, Carly explained how Mia had invited Trent and his parents over to the Cosentinos for a dinner and game night. That's the real reason she was having a girl's night with Maddie. Additionally, Carly wanted to gush about her a date to another girl—even if that meant Maddie. Plus, she knew Sophia would love to hear the details of her date as well as the interesting couple next to them, as Maddie was sure to leave Sophia high and dry in the areas of dating.

Pilot was just glad he got to spend a little extra time with Carly, as the trip to his house was longer from the restaurant, than it was to Carly's. It was a nice bonus to have his perfect girlfriend's hand intertwined in his during the walk, and he soaked up every minute.

After kissing Pilot goodnight on Maddie's doorstep, she stepped into the kitchen where Sophia was waiting with a tray full of fresh baked cookies.

"Cookies for gossip?" Carly asked, raising her eyebrows.

Sophia smiled coyly. Carly laughed in good-spirits, and replayed the details of her date, as well as an exact description of Asbury's finest fine-dining experience, as the ads ran. Sophia seemed to enjoy eating up the gossip more than the cookies.

Which was perfect for Maddie. She came downstairs, fresh from showering, to find a tray full of warm cookies and blessedly only caught the end of Carly's date, which consisted of a detailed description of the Post Officer's date. Maddie couldn't care less about that, so she pushed that information out of her mind, as she pushed the cookies into her mouth.

When Sophia was satiated with gossip, Maddie and Carly made their way upstairs to Maddie's room.

"I have some more tea to spill," Carly confided, as she sat down eagerly on the end of Maddie's bed.

Maddie expertly suppressed an eyeroll, and joined her pal on her bed.

As Carly revealed Alexis' rejection from

Cornelious, Maddie felt her heart lighten. She was proud that her best friend had not fallen for the succubus that was Alexis Johnson.

Carly grinned, "I knew you'd be happy."

Maddie shrugged indifferently, "Of course. You are too. Alexis is a horrible human being—and that's putting it nicely."

"Uh-huh…What about you and Eric Henry?"

A confused look crossed over Maddie's features. "What about us?"

"So, there is an US!" Carly victoriously boomed.

"What? NO! You literally just asked about me and him."

"Well… he's clearly interested in you. Dating you, I mean. Ever consider giving him a chance?"

Maddie felt the blood rush into her cheeks. "Number one—he's never even asked me out nor came anywhere close to that. Number two—he's not my, um, type. Sure, Eric is nice, and cute enough— I admit—but he's not a smart guy, and cares way too much about appearances. He just doesn't have that… that… thing, ya know?" Maddie explained all of this in the professional manner of giving a class presentation.

"Basically…." Carly drawled out, and started examining her nails, seemingly avoiding eye contact, "You're saying he's not Cornelious." Carly quickly fixed her gaze to Maddie's, who stammered and begun speaking a mile a minute in return.

"What? No! That's not what I meant." Maddie's heartbeat quickened and she felt her nerves light up. "Neal is Neal, I don't even… there's no… Besides, let's not forget he DID at least consider dating Alexis. I mean, they've kissed, and even went to that dumb dance together last year. He's even stood up for her before to us."

"So?" Carly asked, fluffing her pillow, and pulling out her orange and pink sunset sleeping bag, which she had recently purchased to stash under Maddie's bed and replace the over worn bean bags. Though she could've slept on the bed, she had become so used to the arrangement of her and Pilot sleeping next to each other on the floor, while Maddie and Cornelious had the bed, that laying on the floor was second nature to her.

"So… if that's the type of girl he's into, then he's not the type of guy I'm into. And that I know for a fact." Maddie leaned back on the bed, and switched on the TV, effectively switching off the conversation.

16

Even if Pilot had not confided in Carly about his conversation with Cornelious—who then revealed everything to Maddie—it was obvious that following week in school that Alexis had moved on. Or at least, that she had temporarily given Cornelious and the gang the cold shoulder. Not that it made a difference in their life, nor did the quartet care. With the Carly's revelation regarding Brett Dull, the gang was in full investigatory gear. In fact, they probably wouldn't have even noticed, if it wasn't for third period AP English.

A few moments after the bell rang, a Willy Wonka look-a-like burst into the room and immediately commenced a story about his latest health ailment—which involved him tripping inside the Hartman Hotel, and resulted in getting his gall bladder removed. Although no one was able to make the connection, they still found themselves laughing at their crazy teacher, Mr. Day. For some odd reason or another, Mr. Day was a more frequent resident of the Asbury Hospital than his own apartment (in the Hartman Hotel). His outlandish stories and consistent tardiness to his own class, made their AP English class one of the more enjoyable ones.

What made today's class even better for Maddie, was that before Mr. Day's arrival Alexis had entered the room and loudly told Ed she would like to trade back seats. Back in September, Alexis had paid Ed one hundred bucks so that she could sit next to Cornelious, as the desks were arranged in pairs. Ed, who greedily accepted the bribe, hadn't realized he was moving next to Brittney Anne Saratelli. Unfortunately for him, she was also surrounded by her minions Sarah and Jewel, and each English class they either discussed ways to impress Alexis or talked trash on everyone in the class. For once in his life, Ed's obnoxious ways were tamed by a constant headache from the trio of girls.

Maddie was lucky to have Peetie sitting next to her, but for once felt that she wouldn't mind having Ed directly behind her. The choice between Ed and Alexis was like choosing between a root canal or open-heart surgery. Both would be painful experiences, but at least one wouldn't mess with your smile.

After changing seats, and before Mr. Day made his frazzled entrance, Alexis made one last point to tell her trio of admirers that she was going on a date with Jason Scott this weekend. Although Cornelious was unmoved and continued to pull out his notebook and pencil, Maddie felt a grin spread across her face and was glad that all was right in the world again.

Later during practice, Jason Scott bragged to the basketball team that he and Alexis had a big date coming up. Most of the guys thought Alexis was pretty hot, and obviously loaded, so they were impressed. Cornelious found himself thanking the Sweet Lord that she had moved on, and laughed. When Jason then asked what was funny about hooking up with a hottie, Cornelious grabbed a rebound, shook his head, and said "Nothing, you two are a match made in… well, a perfect match."

Jason shrugged, not always understanding his friend, but also proud of himself for securing such a popular date. For even Jason didn't really feel any pull of attraction towards the good-looking red-head. In fact, he barely knew much about her, even though they had grown up together in Asbury. Regardless, he viewed this date as another ladder rung climbed in his quest to be the most popular one in high school. Plus, he knew his father would be proud.

Carly, who sat through cheer practice with Alexis boasting that she was dating a professional football player's son (everyone knows Jason, just say his name, Carly thought), desperately wanted to share the news with her friends. But she also didn't want to bring up gossip on Alexis—when it wasn't necessary. She was trying her best to distance herself from Alexis, and Pilot had told her to train her brain to clear any unwanted thoughts. It actually worked, if she kept reminding herself to work at it. Plus, she realized, with the way both Jason and Alexis brag, the whole town probably knew they were dating.

Coincidentally, cheer practice and the boys' basketball practice had ended at the same time (the girls' team had off today). Cornelious pushed through the double doors of the gym, to see Carly bent over and packing up her gear into her cheerleading bag.

"Hey, Carly!" Cornelious jogged over to walk with his friend.

Carly turned and smiled. "Hey! How was practice?"

"Same old, same old. We're not doing too many sprints anymore, seeing as playoffs are next week."

Stepping into her gray and red sweatpants, Carly grinned, "Oh man. That means you and Maddie are about to go full beast mode, huh?"

Cornelious laughed and agreed that he and Maddie were known to zone everything out when it came to playoffs. Luckily for him, he shared every class with Maddie, and while she never neglected her schoolwork during such times, he could not claim the same. However, he also knew Maddie always had his back, which left his with no worries—other than playoffs.

As the two walked outside, Carly saw her dad's black car parked out front. "Want a ride?"

Seeing as the gray sky looked as if it was about to explode with snow, Cornelious readily agreed. The duo stepped to the car and were surprised to see the whole Cosentino clan in the SUV.

"Uh, hey guys." Cornelious greeted the family, not sure if a ride home was still an option.

"Cornelious! Oh, come on in. We're heading to the Petrozza's now for dinner!" Mrs. Cosentino beamed from the passenger seat, holding a tray of a delicious smelling dessert in her lap.

"And before you object, we know you practically live there, son… so climb aboard!" Mr. Cosentino laughed.

Mia slid over and made room for the two teens to join.

Carly and Cornelious looked at each other nervously when Mr. Cosentino told them that Mia and Trent had some big news to share and wanted to tell the two families together.

"I hope they're not pregnant," Carly whispered low, so only Cornelious could hear.

Sensing her sister's thoughts, Mia grumbled, "And no, we're not pregnant or anything."

Cornelious felt his own face go red, but was surprised when Mr. and Mrs. Cosentino just laughed in reply.

When the Cosentinos, plus Cornelious, had arrived they weren't surprised to find that Pilot and Mrs. Owens were in attendance too. After a few minutes of corralling all the kids to the dinner table, Trent and Mia stood, holding hands, at the top of the table.

"So, as you know we've been dating for a year now," Trent began, looking uncomfortable, "and we're heading off to college next year…"

The parents exchanged glances, but patiently waited for the announcement to unfold.

"And, we just wanted to let everyone know, together…" the young couple looked at each other and grinned.

"That we're both going to be Blue Hens!" Mia

proclaimed excitedly.

The parents clapped, and congratulated the two, while Alec voiced the question everyone younger than him was wondering themselves, “So you’re turning into animals?”

Trent laughed, “No, bro. We both got into University of Delaware and are going to college together!”

The rest of dinner and dessert pleasantly flew by, with parental advice already spilling out from both sides.

As the last of the dessert was gobbled up, a “DING!” from Pilot’s pocket broke the silence.

Pulling out his phone, Pilot grumbled an apology, and quick eye contact with his friends revealed he had something to share. Thanking their parents for the delicious meal, the foursome quickly placed their plates in the sink and asked if they could head to Pilot’s.

After quickly crossing the lawn, and finding themselves securely in Pilot’s room, Cornelious inquired first, “What’s up, Pi?”

“I just got an alert from Asbury PD of another case of money going missing at Asbury Bank.”

Without another word, the gang settled down in their usual spots, and waited for the projector to roll down, and their Mystery Machine program to start up. Within seconds they found themselves looking over the footage from Asbury Bank, during the time that the money went missing. Unfortunately, they also found themselves at another stalemate. For the video footage showed nothing out of the ordinary.

“Man, maybe the thief really is Houdini.” Maddie frustratingly sat back against the bed, unable to think of a next step.

"And we're sure it's not an online crime? Like a wire transfer we can trace?" Carly asked.

"No, there's just n—" Pilot began, but was quickly cut off by his friend.

Cornelious sprung up and stood next to the screen. "Wait a second! Replay the tape."

Shrugging, Pilot pressed rewind on the remote.

"That's it!" Cornelious clapped his hands, and faced his friends. Pausing for dramatic effect, he pointed to the screen, "This tape looks frozen.'"

"Frozen?" both girls asked in unison.

"Yeah. Like someone pressed pause, but only for about a minute... maybe less. Look," he grabbed the remote and rewound it. For about a minute, Cornelious pointed to various customers and tellers who didn't move a single muscle.

"Even those plants by the AC vent aren't moving!" Carly exclaimed, noting the extremely still plants in the corner of the screen.

Pilot's eyes widened to the size of grapefruits. "You're right! I can't even imagine the technology that would be involved in this. They could be using a top-grade signal jammer—possibly even military grade."

Cornelious voiced everyone's thoughts over Pilot's use of the word technology, "Would Rhodes Technology have access to that type of tech?"

Pilot mulled the question over, but couldn't say for certain whether or not Rhodes had high-enough quality jammers. "We could check it out, but I kind of doubt they'd have anything this serious."

Maddie didn't have to say a word to know her friends were all experiencing the same tingling sensation signifying that they had found a break in the case.

"If it is a jammer, which it seems like it is, then how do the police not realize it?" Carly questioned.

"It's a very subtle job… look, the bank clock in the corner of the tape continues counting—AMAZING." Pilot's jaw just about dropped, as the rest admitted it was difficult to see the video itself was frozen, when the time was still ticking away clearly in the corner.

"It's almost like an optical illusion," Cornelious murmured.

"Once again, all clues point to Houdini as the thief." Maddie half-joked.

17

The first week of March meant spring was coming soon, but for the winter athletes it meant playoffs had officially begun. It also was Maddie's sixteenth birthday, but she had made sure to tell everyone that she didn't want a Sweet Sixteen, as she saw no value in that number. She wasn't getting her license until next year, and couldn't vote until the following one. And although Brady's made a special dessert for her and the gang, after Jenna Owens informed them of her birthday when the foursome walked in on March 7th, everyone else honored her wishes.

Well, almost everyone. Although he didn't throw her a party, Cornelious pointed out that it was called Sweet Sixteen for a reason, and he stopped into Tyler's Tantalizing Treats to procure a rare peanut butter chocolate truffle, that they even painted golden and attached wings to mimic the Golden Snitch from Harry Potter.

After her parents had sang her Happy Birthday and devoured a few pizza pies, Cornelious presented her with her delicious gift. With wide eyes, she thanked him profusely, but then felt bad eating the whole treat in front of him. Laughing, he pulled out his own Snitch from a separate box and the two raised their snitches in cheers, leaving no crumbs behind.

Even if Pilot and Carly couldn't keep the recent break in the case from their minds, they were amazed that Cornelious and Maddie were able to completely shut out everything and focus solely on the games ahead of them. Thus, the couple took it upon themselves to investigate Rhodes Technology. Unfortunately, just as Pilot suspected, the few signal-jammers that were in stock were such low-grade that Pilot doubted if they had the capacity to block a basic phone call from leaving a five meter-radius. They definitely couldn't imperceptibly freeze federal bank footage.

By the time the second week of March had rolled around, both basketball teams found themselves in the state quarterfinals, and by the end of the week, the girls were on their way to a state final. Unfortunately, the boys' team fell short (by four), to senior-heavy Jupiter High, and their hopes of bringing it all home came to a sudden end.

That Friday, Maddie and girls' team felt like they were floating on cloud nine—for teachers and fellow students offered congratulations and good luck greetings throughout the day. Cornelious was excited for his friend, but still felt the hollow ache of losing the night before. For that reason, most of his fellow teammates decided to stay home or spend the day at the Luxurious Lady penthouse, with Jason covering all costs of course.

Even though the idea of skipping sounded tempting, Cornelious would rather be surrounded by his best friends, than reminded all day of their loss at the Scott's. Nevertheless, throughout the day most of the school made a point to stop by and tell Cornelious how great his past season had been—Coach Baruff even pulled him aside to inform him that he was well on the way to shattering Asbury's boys' basketball points and steals records. In fact, he could even top one thousand points in the second game next year—something Maddie had already calculated and excitedly told him already.

While personal success is always something to be proud of, and with half of his high school career in the books, Cornelious was hoping to accept a scholarship to college (in the increasingly near future), the desire to win a team championship still burned deep, and he would've traded all those stats for a State Championship.

Sitting down with his tray in front of him, Pilot watched as his friend pushed his food around his tray, rather than stuff his face. Trying to cheer him up, Pilot told a story of how Jason and Hannah had gotten into a heated argument in his English class about whether 'Animal Farm' was a work of fiction. Hannah believed it was real, as it was written 'clear as day' in a book they were reading in school, whereas Jason exasperatingly pointed out that animals can't talk nor possess the ability to run a farm. Carly asked where the teacher was during all of this, and Pilot said they revealed they had had a sub.

The gang burst into laughter and Cornelious felt his spirits continue to lift. Especially when, as lunch was coming to a close, Jazz and his band walked over to their table, and congratulated him on his 'epic' season. Jazz even patted Cornelious on the back, before leaving the cafeteria.

"He really seems to have taken Johanna's advice to heart," Maddie noted, between bites of her pb and j sandwich.

Cornelious smiled, for as long as he had known the musician, Jazz had always disliked him based on his address. It was nice to realize that people could change and things like money didn't always have the final say—as much as Jeremiah Gibbz preached the opposite.

After lunch, Carly sped away to meet with her fellow cheerleaders about some routines and special additions they could make for Sunday's state final. Carly wanted to make it extra special for Maddie and her team.

Cornelious, Maddie, and Pilot walked from the lunchroom to their lockers, discussing Cornelious' season high triple-double last night, and how next year the guys' team were a shoe-in for the finals. Cornelious argued that nothing is guaranteed, but just fantasizing about next season with his buds helped ease his pain at last night's loss.

"Hey, Maddie! Wait up!" an excited voice called from behind them.

The trio turned to see Bo Dylans making his way to them. Pilot smirked, when he saw Bo's brother, Anthony shoot daggers at them. Ever since Carly turned Anthony down, Pilot noticed how Anthony had either avoided the gang or shown outright anger towards them. That was fine with Pilot.

As Bo edged by Maddie's side, and walked with her to her next class, he regaled her with his spot-on impressions of her teammates and those she had recently defeated. Admittedly, Maddie was impressed that he had paid so much attention to the game, and was so talented at character impersonations. Blushing, he revealed how he had attended theater camp for the past few summers and that was why he hadn't been in Asbury during vacation.

Hoping she was somewhat of a good actor herself, she replied, "Oh, that's why I never see you in the summer," as she didn't want to hurt the kid's feelings. Clearly, he wanted her to know the reason why she didn't see him in the summer. Not that she would've hung out with him anyway… the two weren't even in the same grade, and she rarely hung out with anyone other than her own gang and various teammates.

Coming up behind Pilot and Cornelious, Eric angrily whispered in his friend's ear, "What's he doing?"

Taking a second, Cornelious realized Eric was referencing Bo and Maddie's conversation. Cornelious smiled and told his worried friend not to stress. "As I said before, there's no need to worry about Bo Dylans and Maddie. She would never go for him… I can't even picture Maddie dating anyone."

Hearing the latter part, Eric scowled at Cornelious, and stalked off down the hall in the opposite direction.

"What's his problem?" Cornelious asked, staring at the fading backside of his friend.

Pilot looked at Cornelious and replied, "It's pretty clear, dude. Eric is way into Maddie. I'm pretty sure even

Maddie has to know by now."

"What? No. How'd you know this?" Cornelious came to an abrupt stop in the middle of the hallway.

Pilot grinned and pulled his friend along to class, "Well, besides having eyes and seeing how obvious it is… my girlfriend is a walking encyclopedia of high school—scratch that, town gossip."

Cornelious considered this and watched Bo walk away smiling. Following his best bud into class, Cornelious tried to imagine Eric Henry or even Bo Dylans dating his best friend. He had to laugh. Maddie was too smart for them, and plus, she never even mentioned dating. And he knew she would definitely confide in him before anyone else. Right?

18

"Gooo-ooo-oood Morning-ing ing layy-dees and gentle, gentle, gentlemen! We sure did-a-lee-doo have an exy-exy-exciting finaly-final last night-ight, alright!" A familiarly, pleasant sing-songy voice sang throughout the halls of Asbury High. Students and teachers alike couldn't contain their smiles for their beloved school secretary. Ex-Broadway superstar Ms. Dugan remembered her tedious, boring high school days—of actively drowning out the school announcements. She vowed to herself when she took the secretary job at Asbury years ago, that no student would ever sit through the same torture she endured. Thus, every announcement—except the rare tragic and extremely sad news—was sung with joy and love.

"We-ee-ee must do-do-da-do our very bestest to

congratulate the girls' successes! Last night-ighty alrighty, proved to be-be a victory-ree in the state final! Nya led the way-ay-ay to the toppity top with oh-I-see, twenty-three…points that is, and adding to the bizz-ness of winning and tallying up the score was from fellow soph-o-more Maddie-ee with sixteen points and five steals—that's real! And let's not forget, quite yet, freshman standout, young Ms. Carmen, who with twelve assists and ten points refused to lose!"

When the announcements ended, the school erupted in applause—as much toward the song Ms. Dugan belted out, as to congratulate the State Championship Girls' Team.

Maddie couldn't get more than a few feet down the hall, without a high-five or a congratulatory greeting. Around this time last year, she couldn't make it more than a few feet down the hall without glares of suspicion or mean words garnered for her mother's arrest. Maddie reflected on how much could change in a year, but wasn't one to dwell on the past and graciously accepted all compliments.

Only Alexis seemed to think today was one of the worst days of school in recent memory. At lunch, Carly even noticed that instead of becoming green with envy, she had finally managed to turn the same color as her hair! Everyone laughed in agreement.

As Maddie sat down next to her friends in Study Hall, Cornelious noticed she seemed less than happy.

"Sick of all the attention?" Cornelious asked, happy to put off graphing linear equations.

"No… well, a little. But's not the attention of our fellow peers that's bothering me… it's Cunningham." Maddie stole a glance over to where the librarian was catching an unfortunate student in a lie about a missing book.

Carly smirked, and Pilot nodded, adding, "She finally caught up to you."

Maddie sighed. "Yeah. And she had Milton with her. They were both saying how proud they were to have a celebrity in book club and now that I my seasons are finished they're thrilled to have me back as a regular member."

"Have you even gone this year, yet?" Cornelious inquired, thinking about how busy they had been and quickly the year had passed.

"Twice. To get the book list in September and then a random meeting in December. But don't worry, Milton keeps me up to date on all the minutes, as that's his new duty this year."

"Too bad you can't back out," Carly murmured, and was glad she wasn't allowed entry into the prestigious book club.

Maddie's eye widened at the very thought of quitting. "I wouldn't even dare."

All four friends shuddered as they recalled the horror stories, passed down by generations, of those who did Cunningham and her sacred book club wrong. It was easier to pardon a death-row sentence—for an air-tight case of a self-confessed serial killer—than to break away from the club amicably, and with a bright future intact. That is unless, of course, your plan is to be the aforementioned inmate.

"Seems I have an hour-long meeting after school today to discuss 'Atlas Shrugged.' I mean, I LOVED that book, but… I need a break from extra-curriculars."

Cornelious put his arm around his best friend and tried to be encouraging. "At least it's only an hour, and Pi and I will hit up Brady's after school and bring you something for the walk home."

Maddie smiled. "Thanks guys. Now I have something more delicious than a discussion on Rand's famous characters to look forward to."

******

Walking in between Cornelious and Pilot, while slurping a delicious homemade Brady's milkshake, Maddie felt relief wash over her. She had survived book club and now actually had free time to dive into their investigation. Although Carly still had cheerleading this year, neither Cornelious nor Maddie played a spring sport and were free to join Pilot in solving the case.

The trio continued to walk into West Asbury and Pilot pointed out the small, yet cozy tan rancher that was home to the most famous Butcher in Asbury—and Asburyans considered, of all the world.

"I swear I could smell fresh, roasting meat every time we pass the Davies'." Cornelious inhaled the air deeply to make his point.

"I know. I'm practically drooling," Maddie drooled.

Pilot laughed. "Just think, Mads. If you marry Milton, your house could smell like this all of the time!"

Maddie laughed. "So, we'd move in with his parents? We all know Milton is no skilled butcher."

Both boys chuckled in agreement, but then Pilot wrinkled his nose, "And probably all of your clothes would smell too. It's amazing Milton and his little sister don't smell like meat."

"It's not like they work with Wolfgang at the Butcher Shop. Plus, his wife probably makes sure he scrubs himself down before entering the house." Maddie pictured the goofy couple, and didn't realize how right she was. Wolfgang's wife, Cassandra, always made him use the outdoor shower before coming in the front door. She was no vegetarian, but after a lifetime of being a Butcher's wife, she needed a meat free space.

Also imagining the same scenario, Pilot added, "That'll be another one of your jobs, scrubbing down Milton. It'd be so romantic," Pilot batted his eyelashes, as both Maddie and Cornelious gagged.

The trio continued laughing at the mental image, although (yet again), Cornelious felt himself forcing the joke. In fact, they very thought of Maddie sitting down to dinner with Milton and his parents made him feel uneasy—to say the least.

"Guys!" Look!" Maddie stopped cold and pointed to the dilapidated Willow Apartment Complex. Although it was in much need of repair and serious landscaping, seeing as it was located in West Asbury town funding tended to pass it right by, year after year. Unfortunately, many hard-working families lived in the brick apartment complex, but had little time or money leftover (after paying an unfairly steep rent to the Johnson family, of course), to put towards beautification.

Cornelious often toyed with the idea of fixing it up himself, but knew his dad would involve himself and probably make the situation worse somehow. He could do it anonymously, but after last year's donation to the

Historical Center, he feared stirring up suspicions. Maybe when he was older and had graduated college, he would make it one of many fixer-upper projects, he argued with himself whenever he passed the rundown area.

Coming back to the present, the two boys followed Maddie's pointed finger and watched as JB and his Pitbulls piled into a crowded first-floor brick apartment.

"No way." Cornelious warned. He didn't need to be to be Professor X to know what his friend was thinking.

"What?!" Pilot and Maddie innocently asked together, their brains in sync.

"I know exactly what you two are thinking. It's too dangerous, and just plain stupid," Cornelious sternly argued.

"Neal," Maddie put her hand on her friend's shoulder. "You know there's a chance they're involved in the missing money. And clearly, they've found a new headquarters."

"And," Pilot cut in, "unless they hit the lotto or all started working—"

"Unlikely," Maddie snorted.

"Then there's no legitimate way they could afford that apartment."

Cornelious sighed, dragging his hand down his face. "Every time we go after them, we have been WRONG! And then they retaliate and we end up escalating the bad blood between us."

While the three friends stood arguing over their next move, a Pitbull deemed 'the Lookout' alerted JB to the trio's proximity to their headquarters. Hence, Cornelious, Maddie, and Pilot were surprised when they heard JB clear his throat, and found the Pitbull leader and three of his felonious gang members behind them.

"Maybe I should welcome you, but I feel like I should just make this short and sweet and ask why you're sneaking around OUR place?" JB crossed his big arms and waited.

"We're not sneaking!" Maddie answered defiantly. "And how is a whole entire, albeit grossly uncared for, apartment complex YOUR place?"

"Do you actually want something?" JB smiled his creepy Cheshire-cat-like smile, ignoring her questioning.

Pilot, deciding they were way past niceties at this point in the game, came right out with it: "How do you afford rent?"

JB eyed the curly-headed dork and honestly answered, "We have investors."

Seeing the truth in his words, but not understanding who would pay the way for the Pitbulls—yet knowing they wouldn't get any more intel—the threesome exchanged glances and silently agreed to leave it. For now.

"Come on. Let's go." Cornelious broke the silence (and the stare down), and turned to go. As Pilot and Maddie followed suite, they heard JB's triumphant chuckle and wondered who would invest in a teenage gang of known troublemakers?

19

Although the sunny skies seemed to thaw out Asbury's mood— for teachers and employees around town could physically be seen skipping to work at times—as March became April, the gang's feelings still mirrored those of winter. The school year was reaching its final marking period, and although criminals don't follow academic school years as their timeline to begin or end a crime spree, the foursome felt the time left to solve their case was running thin.

Simply put, all four were stuck. Maddie and Cornelious made time to work out together in the beautiful weather, but their workouts were more quiet than usual for each was also working through their thoughts regarding the investigation. Even Carly's cheer coach pulled her aside to address her low-levels of pep. Pilot, after firmly verifying the bank's tapes were being jammed by a remote military-grade signal jammer, frustratingly scoured the web for recent purchases of such equipment to the area. To no avail.

That Saturday morning, it had decided to pour. Which meant that Maddie was stuck at home babysitting, as Trent and her parents had a video conference with Trent's new football coach at the University of Delaware. Knowing the trouble and overall ruckus their youngest were bound to make, they headed to the Auto Shop for some peace and quiet.

Also finding himself stuck at home, was Pilot. His mother and Mr. Chanaki viewed this rainy day as a perfect opportunity to get to know each other even better. Thus, a family game day was declared, with all three having a blast.

The sudden change in plans of their West-Asbury half, meant Carly and Cornelious met up at Molly and Erin's Music Emporium feeling half-charged. They had planned to use this opportunity to fully delve into the investigation.

"I'm just saying, all this money goes missing and JB and his little gang suddenly find themselves under the good will of investors? In a new, fully-furnished apartment?" Carly incredulously shook her head, as she scanned through multi-colored vinyl albums, which weren't even really for sale. Although MEME'S was a throwback to old-school music stores, it also sold music equipment as well as offered the newest advances (and advice) in today's music-world. Mostly, people came to hang out and discover the latest trends or hot single. Or to meet up with one of the most famous couples in town, Molly and Erin. As world-famous retired rockers, the two women knew how to entertain.

Cornelious disagreed. "I know it looks suspicious, and maybe we should try to find out who's giving them that much money—and why… but… I just don't think they're involved in the Asbury Bank's missing money. First of all, it's way too complex of a crime for them. And second of all, every single time we go down that alley, we've always been wrong and they've been innocent."

Carly sighed, "I don't know if we should ever call them innocent. They do some pretty shady things."

Before the two could continue their conversation, a beaming blonde, dressed to the nines in a yellow pencil skirt and black blouse stepped up to them.

"Peetie!" Carly squealed with delight. Everyone was always glad to see Peetie, although with her busy schedule and current role as President of Student Council (two years straight!), it was becoming more and more difficult to see their friend.

"Hey guys! I feel like it's been forever… this year has been crazy! I can tell you horror stories of trying to rebalance Asbury High's budget! Coste has been Trump-like in releasing the financial records."

Everyone laughed. Stepping up from behind his sister, Jazz groaned, "Please don't tell me you're starting up with Student Council mumbo-jumbo again."

Peetie smiled and play-smacked her twin on the shoulder. "They were very interested to hear how we rebalanced various aspects of their everyday school life."

After a few minutes of getting caught up, the twins left the two on their own again, as Jazz's bandmates entered the store.

"Does Jazz always carry that guitar with him? I

mean, even in the hallways its slung around his shoulder," Carly wondered to Cornelious.

Cornelious shrugged, and pulled out a long Bob Marley hoodie, with dreadlocks attached to the hood. "This is awesome!"

"No." Carly warned, foreseeing her friend wearing such a fashion-atrocity made her stomach turn. "Didn't you already get your fill of dreadlocks from Halloween this year?"

Cornelious laughed, and the two got in line to ask the clerk about a SONOS speaker Cornelious was interested in.

"I'm JUST SAYING," came a loud, obnoxious voice from a few people ahead of them in line, "that I shouldn't have to pay you full price. For people like you the difference between twenty and twenty-five dollars is nothing. You've probably never held a real twenty-dollar bill in your life."

Before the bullied and embarrassed sales clerk could stammer a reply, the nasty voice continued, "'Cuz if you have seen an actual twenty, I bet you wouldn't be wearing those same rags that I'm sure can be found in any trash can around town."

Not one to stand idly by while someone is being bullied, Cornelious and Carly eyed each other and stepped out of line to confront the jerk.

Little to their surprise, did they see a red-headed, curly-haired girl shaking her fist and berating the cashier.

"Alexis, you're the one who should be embarrassed. You've never worked a day in your life, have all the money in the world, and still can't afford a shirt for twenty-five dollars." Carly snapped at Alexis, as Alexis spun to face her confronter.

About to say something nasty, Alexis stopped short and her face paled, as she saw Cornelious was standing there, looking disgusted. "I can't believe I thought you changed… you're as cold-hearted as ever."

"Cornelious," Carly crossed her arms, "that's kind of you to even assume she has a heart."

Too mortified to think of a reply, or perhaps too shocked at being exposed for who she truly is in front of her lifelong crush, Alexis dropped her shopping bag on the counter and ran out of the store.

"Thank you," whispered the shy, embarrassed MEME clerk.

"There's nothing to it," Carly stated, "That was an example of a person who only feels good about themselves by putting others down."

Cornelious smiled at the blushing young girl and added, "She won't get far in life, or at least won't ever be happy. Believe me, anyone would rather be you than her."

The cashier smiled, and visibly brightened. Surely, if these two good-looking, kind-hearted, and confident teenagers saw more value in her than in that rude customer, they couldn't be wrong.

Carly leaned over in collusion, "Plus, we all despise her." The young cashier giggled, and the two turned to get back in line.

"No way guys! You two earned the right to cut in front of us." Cornelious and Carly smiled, and were happy to see Owen, Tyler, and Scott of The Nooks, standing behind them, each holding a piece of paper.

"Thanks! We're really just here to ask a question, it won't take more than a minute," Carly assured them.

After the cashier expertly directed Cornelious to which SONOS to purchase, the two turned back to Jazz's bandmates. "You guys are awesome! We just have to say," Carly admitted.

The three brothers (ranging in age from Junior year at Asbury High to eighth grade), all smiled. "We just do our best—Jazz is the real mastermind," Tyler, the youngest, answered.

"Yeah well, no doubt Jazz is good, but all of you guys together make the band unbelievable," Cornelious stated.

As Carly and Cornelious continued talking to Owen (the middle sibling, and also in their grade), they overheard the cashier explaining how the trio would have to wait a week to purchase their highly-desired new band equipment.

"Seriously?" Scott, the eldest of the three, asked incredulously. "We've been saving for three years to update our equipment, and just yesterday we saw you guys had the pieces we wanted."

The cashier shook her head sadly, "I'm sorry… it's just with this 'Siblings Sale' we're running this weekend, another pair of siblings came in earlier and bought the exact pieces you guys had in mind."

The brothers looked stunned. Owen hung his head and announced that "we'll have to tell grams and gramps the hundred each they just sent us to buy the goods isn't going to cut it."

"And in their last letter they sent us last weekend, they seemed so excited to contribute to the band," Tyler added.

Sympathizing, the cashier wrote a note and handed it to the brothers. "Tell you what, I'll consider this a raincheck and when it comes in next week, I'll put it aside and still honor this weekend's Siblings Sale."

The brothers brightened and promised to come the second she called, as she blushingly handed Tyler her cell number. Tyler smiled and shyly asked if he could text her even if it wasn't work-related.

Sensing something that only girls seem to notice, Carly grinned and took Cornelious by the arm, leading him away.

"I can't believe it," Cornelious muttered.

"I know! What are the odds that another set of siblings wanting to buy the same instruments? Especially in this small of a town. It's kind of fishy."

"No, not that," Cornelious said.

"Oh… yeah I know! I could totally see Tyler hanging out with that clerk. I think she's a freshman, I know I know I've seen her around the freshmen lockers."

Cornelious smiled at his friend's strong memory and love for all things gossip-related. "I was talking about how Alexis could be so cruel to such a nice person."

Carly sighed and shook her head, "Maddie's been saying it for years… I've always tried to keep the peace, since I cheer with her virtually every day. But, there's no hiding the monster under the cheer uniform anymore."

Cornelious laughed and agreed. "I guess I'm not as good a judge of character… Maddie said as much when she brought up Rachel Maer—that was disastrous."

Carly's eyes twinkled. "You're a boy. It's not so

much a question of being a bad judge of character, as it is about just stopping at the surface. You know, you see something pretty, and reach for it—even if the inside is worthless or rotten."

Cornelious thought it over. "That's pretty deep."

As the two friends dashed out into the rain and took Cornelious' limo to Maddie's (hoping to aid her in babysitting before Daniel and Shannon burned down Asbury), Cornelious made a new vow to himself. He was going to be more aware and not so easily fooled when it came to, as Carly called it, pretty things.

Carly snapped him out of his thoughts, and pulled him over to her side of the limousine. "Neal! Look!"

Pressed against the window, Cornelious squinted through the rain, to see a lanky, balding man, with a fierce mustache, shaking Chief Chip's hands, as he left the Police Department and stepped into the rain. "It looks like the Police brought Brett Dull into the station," Cornelious said.

"Yeah, but that looked to be a friendly handshake… maybe they were clearing him," Carly pondered aloud.

Both teens sat back in their seat, and contemplated what it could mean that Brett Dull was clearly at the Asbury PD today, but appeared to be leaving on good terms. Was he really innocent? Or was there more to the skinny man than met the eye?

20

Later that night, the students of Asbury High convened in the West Asbury junkyard. No, they were not aiming to collect garbage, nor were they there to rally to protect the environment and begin a recycling movement (for Peetie had a plan already in motion in regards to that).

On this wet and dark, yet mildly warm evening, the teenagers of Asbury were gathering in the ten-foot high junkpile, manned by self-proclaimed Junkyard Dog Johnny. Luckily for the gang, Johnny remembered them from last year—as he was known to remember faces and only interrogate freshmen—allowing them to pass through the oversized tire that marked the entrance. As always, the gang was impressed by their surroundings. Even though it was not their first time in the concert hall, or anti-concert hall as Asbury's true concert hall was located in Pecunia Palace, they were stunned by its enormity nonetheless.

The self-constructed hall was more of a large room, mostly consisting of a large dirt-packed dance floor. However, as with most hang-out spots, there were bean bags and ez-chairs strewn all over the room, with the focus being the wooden stage situated at the end of the hall. The lights shone brightly, and tonight the concession stand was packed. Apparently, the addition of Doritos and pretzels doubled their non-existent sales. The only rule that was actually enforced here, mostly by the bands playing each night, was that no alcohol was to be sold or permitted inside. The bands finally found a place they could play whenever they wished, and they didn't want the adults of the town to have a legitimate reason to take their haven from them. Amazingly, those who attended the concerts complied without hesitation. In fact, most of the upperclassmen viewed the rule as an excuse to host an after party.

When the foursome not only made their way inside, but also found a prime location halfway out on the floor (they still wanted to be able to converse while listening to the bands play), they caught each other up on earlier events. After all day babysitting and playing games, Pilot and Maddie had goofy stories—as well as almost-horror stories too. Those twins got into more trouble than Bonnie and Clyde.

Carly and Cornelious described seeing Mr. Dull exiting the Police Station, seemingly on friendly terms with Chip. Pilot and Maddie exchanged glances, and all four knew they'd be investigating this topic more thoroughly once they left the concert later on. Carly also hurriedly detailed the scene that played out at MEME's, and Maddie's smile couldn't have shone any brighter. Now Cornelious saw the truth behind that two-faced redhead.

"Now that's a smile that lights up this whole junkpile," a playful voice laughed from behind the group.

They turned to see Eric Henry behind them, holding out water bottles for each. Thanking him, the five of them huddled together as the bands began to play. The Dylans Brothers opened and did okay. They had two songs that really got everyone going, but the other two were easily forgettable, if not boring. The real reason to come out to tonight's Battle of the Bands was to hear and see the Nooks perform. Jazz's band was the best band to ever originate in Asbury, and everyone knew they'd be hearing their name on the Grammy stage in the future.

Because of their popularity, they performed last, leaving three other bands to play in between the Dylans' opening act and the Nooks' closing one.

As the third band began their set-list, Maddie felt a tap on her shoulder and turned to face Bo Dylans. He was clearly very proud of himself, as his swagger was evident from his face.

"Great job, Bo. That new equipment you mentioned you were getting looked sweet," Maddie honestly complimented. "And for your first time performing, you guys looked like pros."

Cornelious, standing next to Maddie, rolled his eyes at his friend's compliments, feeling they were exaggerated. He noticed Eric tighten his jaw and glare, as he watched Bo and Maddie's conversation.

"Thanks. I was nervous, but this here is my lucky ring, and it really helps keeps me focused and on point." Bo gestured to his hand, and the bronze pinky ring he was sporting.

Maddie leaned in to look at the offered hand, and Bo swooped down, lips puckered for a kiss! Sensing rather than seeing this coming, Maddie turned her head, and the kiss planted sloppily on her cheek.

"Oh, um thanks." Maddie stepped back, right into Cornelious' side.

Realizing his mistake, Bo bashfully muttered an apology and hastily disappeared into the crowd. Maddie quickly wiped the slobbery remains of the kiss from her face, and turned to her stunned friends. Pilot and Carly chuckled outright, while Eric had stalked off somewhere else. Cornelious' fists were clenched by his side, as he stared after Bo's disappearing figure. What would he have done if Bo had actually kissed Maddie on the lips? Just the thought alone enraged Cornelious.

"Well, that was awkward." Maddie pointed out laughing, as she faced her friends.

"He's probably been building up to that for weeks," Carly stated, still laughing.

Pilot nodded, "When he turned away, he looked like you had spit on his face!"

Maddie felt bad for embarrassing Bo, but there was no way she was going to let him kiss her. She hoped he had gotten the hint that she wasn't into him, and was assured by his sudden departure that he understood.

Cornelious was the only one who didn't comment or laugh off the incident, as Carly was keenly aware.

However, she knew better than to say anything, and the gang turned their attention back to the stage.

Predictably, the Nooks beat everyone else, followed by a group of Seniors jumping on stage to announce the whereabouts of the after party. Tired from the long day, the foursome decided to trek back to Maddie's and sleep there.

After Carly and Pilot had set up their sleeping bags, and snuggled in close, Maddie and Cornelious crashed on Maddie's bed. Although an original Twilight Zone episode was playing on the TV in the background, the foursome talked about the concert, and whatever drama Carly had witnessed. Ninety percent of what Carly divulged to them in regards to what took place at the concert, they had completely missed.

"And the Dylans Brothers… I've been thinking," Carly began.

Cornelious remembered Bo leaning in to kiss Maddie, and felt his face flush with anger. He did **not** want to relive that moment, even if his three best friends found it comical. Lucky for him, Carly's mind was wandering in a different direction.

"How is it they were able to afford their equipment? I know it's the same one that Scott, Owen, and Tyler were trying to buy… and didn't they just have two-thousand dollars stolen from them earlier this year?"

It may have sounded like an innocent enough question to amateur minds, but this group of teenage sleuths began to suspect foul play.

Cornelious, eager to throw the Dylans brothers under the bus suggested, half-jokingly, "Maybe they're the ones stealing the bank money."

For a few moments no one spoke.

"Maybe that's something we should be looking into," Pilot ominously responded.

21

Although the gang was eager to start investigating the Dylans brothers and Brett Dull, as well as stake out the bank right away, their week was filled with tests, papers, and the overall busyness of high school life. Cornelious still felt relieved when he saw Alexis actively avoiding him, and opting to spend her time with Jason. In fact, Jason looked more and more miserable each day and Cornelious wondered if he should give him some friendly advice in regards to his choice of girlfriend. But, Cornelious reasoned to himself, Jason wasn't one to accept advice (as he viewed it as others telling him what to do—including from his coaches and teachers). Not to mention that his current number one goal in life to be the most popular man in school probably included dating a good-looking popular cheerleader, or something along those lines. So, Cornelious kept his mouth shut and focused on his schoolwork and the investigation.

For the first time since they started looking into this crime, the foursome actually felt they were making some headway. Maddie was tempted to recommend that they take off on Friday to stake out the bank a day early, but she knew she'd feel guilty about missing school. Plus, there was no guarantee the bank thieves would even strike then—or even at all. They weren't even one hundred percent sure themselves that they were on the right path. If their gut instincts hadn't been so clutch in the past, the group might have given up on this case altogether, as it was surely much more tech-friendly (much to Pilot's delight), than real-live-in-your-face-action that they were used to.

"Okay, so immediately after school is done, my parents are picking up Pilot and me, and we're going to a play over in Dublin Township," Carly explained to the gang, as she stretched out in their shared seventh period gym class. "So, I think we have to postpone investigating until tomorrow."

Maddie breathed out in frustration, but knew that realistically nothing could be done tonight, other than rehashing of the same old, tired facts.

"Okay boys and girls! Time for another Battle Royale!" thundered the good-looking, dark-haired gym teacher Mr. Anjelow as he took his place in front of the amused group of sophomores. In his mid-fifties, Mr. Anjelow easily looked twenty years younger. Perhaps it was because he still spent every summer on the West Coast, participating in athletic tournaments and various outdoor endeavors with his equally active wife. Thirty years ago, the two had even met at a Battle of the Sexes competition, which was the only time that such an event resulted in an undeniable tie. In fact, the tie between the two competitors led to a different kind of tie, as they quickly realized their mutual attraction and tied the knot in an outdoor, obstacle course wedding ceremony.

As a gym teacher at Asbury High, Mr. Anjelow's love of competition, specifically gender battles, meant multiple, various girls vs boys events throughout the year. Today there was a giant puzzle on one side of the room, and a long rope hanging from the ceiling on the other side. Drawing randomly, Mr. Anjelow smiled as he chose Peetie vs Jason for the puzzle, and Maddie vs Ed or the rope climb. Cornelious and Eric outwardly groaned, knowing this would be a blowout victory for the girls.

And after only five minutes had passed, their prediction proved right on par. Maddie had climbed up the rope and rang the bell signaling victory, before Ed had even climbed a foot—he was so busy smack-talking he hadn't even realized Maddie had begun. On the other side, Jason watched in awe as Peetie wound her hair tightly into a ponytail, and easily pieced together down a nine-piece tangram. Peetie smiled shyly at her opposition when he extended his hand in honest congratulations, and even commented, under his breath, that her hair looked nice pulled back.

The girls all cheered, as the boys ran the losing lap, with Pilot bringing up the rear and wishing there could be a computer-based challenge, or at least that he could get voted onto the girls' team somehow.

****

That Saturday morning, at the break of dawn, Carly, Cornelious, Pilot and Maddie met up across the street from the bank, in front of the Fire Department, and went over their plan. Each of the four would take two virtually undetectable Pilot-made cameras, and stick them on each of the two teller booths. Knowing the odds were against them that they would actually catch the crook red-handed while in the bank, they had agreed this was the best course of action. Plus, this way they weren't likely to be hauled in for questioning by Asbury's finest about why four high schoolers would hang around a bank on their day off.

Once the gear was in place and successfully up and running, the gang quickly made their way across town to the Gibbz mansion. Since Jeremiah was at City Hall going over some new plan to possibly add another holiday to the summer fun, and cash in on shoobie-dollars, Nancy decided to host a spa day at home with some close friends. Hence, the foursome was temporarily stunned when they burst through the front door and saw Nancy Gibbz, Mrs. Heston, Mrs. Scott, two other women AND Nancy's beloved cat Howie, covered completely in only an avocado-toxic-purging mix from head to toe. Luckily, the five women and Howie were also lying face down on massage tables—so none of the gang were stuck with an even worse image for life.

Apparently, the women also had the highest caliber ear plugs in and didn't notice the sudden appearance (and gagging noises), of the four teenagers as they scurried up the stairs to the safety of Cornelious' room. After exploding into laughter, the gang settled down and quickly got down to business.

When a half hour had passed with no action, Maddie and Cornelious laced up their sneakers and headed outdoors.

"It's nice to have some alone time, you know," Carly smiled over to her boyfriend, who was currently hunched over his laptop.

Pilot mumbled in reply, but was too focused on the screen to comment further.

Raising herself up on her elbows, as she laid across Cornelious' bed, Carly sighed, "You know, when I recommended that Maddie and Cornelious go for a run to let out their nervous energy, I was also thinking about us."

Pilot nodded, and was about to zoom in on some more footage, when his laptop closed in front of his eyes.

"The point of recording everything is so that we don't have to watch it live." Carly's hand held the PC closed, and she raised her eyebrows at her cute, albeit frustrating boyfriend.

Pilot breathed out and ran his hair through his wild curls. "You're right… I'm an idiot." He reached for Carly and pulled her onto his lap. Both teens felt a thrill go through them as they leaned in and kissed each other. Although both had only ever kissed each other, they couldn't imagine anyone else's lips making them feel so… electric. As they pulled closer at each other, they heard footsteps coming up the stairs, and the voice of their two best friends coming closer.

"They're back this soon?" Pilot complained, as the couple detached themselves from each other.

"Looks like we'll have to continue this later," Carly

promised, and Pilot blushed.

"Did we miss anything?" Maddie asked but, noting her friends' red faces, realized they probably had been thinking even less of the footage than she had.

Cornelious laughed and told his favorite family robot to order some pizza and fries, for this was clearly going to be a long day.

While waiting for the food to arrive, Pilot projected the uploaded the footage onto the wall in front of Cornelious' bed, while Cornelious and Maddie took turns showering in Cornelious' spa-like bathroom.

"Man, every time I shower here I forget I'm in Asbury. It's like some European getaway—or at least what I'd imagine that to be like."

"Well, that's what my dad modeled the bathrooms after, so it makes sense."

A few hours after the pizza arrived, and numerous card games played, Cornelious jumped up and yelled at the video "AHA! We caught ya!"

"What?"

"Who?"

"Is that…"?"

Cornelious smiled and couldn't believe how happy he felt to spot Bo Dylans, dressed up in quite the disguise, entering the bank. In fact, if Cornelious hadn't been secretly hoping to spot Bo, he most likely would not have realized the elderly, stooping man in a bowler hat and graying beard, was indeed his classmate.

"Are you sure?" Carly questioned hesitantly.

"One hundred percent… Pilot zoom in on his fingers and turn up the volume." Cornelious glanced at

Maddie to see her reaction, and he was doubly satisfied to see her excitement at catching Bo Dylans in action.

"Look!" Cornelious pointed to Bo's hand, "That's the lucky ring he was showing off at the Battle of the Bands!"

The group nodded in agreement and listened to the conversation between the teller and the expertly disguised Bo.

"Good morning, young missy. Aren't you looking quite beautiful today?" Bo crooned in a perfect imitation of an elderly man.

The teller blushed and asked how she could be of service today.

"Well, my son asked me to make a substantial withdrawal from his account—he's been a little edgy over the recent, uh, banking issues. I assured him the money is safest where it is, but you know young folk."

The teller sighed and nodded in assent, "I just need some ID, your withdrawal slip, and since it's not your primary account you'll need to answer some security questions."

Bo clapped his hands together and enthusiastically agreed. "But of course, we don't want just anyone pulling money out from our accounts…now, here is my slip—I signed it earlier—and as you can see my name is actually on the account."

The teller ran the slip through the usual security measures and the gang wasn't surprised to see that the signatures matched up exactly. Though they didn't know how Bo had managed to copy Mr. Simonson's signature so accurately, they vowed to find out.

When it came to the security questions, Bo didn't even blink. He was even able to recount how the family feline, Senor Handsome (an answer to a question), was recovering marvelously from his latest Vet adventure. That's when the gang realized how professionally the Dylans brothers worked these thefts. Bo clearly knew every aspect of the Simonson family life. It was eerie.

Before clicking off the screen, or replaying it, the gang watched as Bo stashed the envelope full of cash in his coat pocket and smugly smiled at the bank's cameras—knowing the exact placement of each!

Maddie noted the obvious, "It looks like Brett Dull is off the hook."

Cornelious nodded, but then remarked, "Unless he is a silent business partner… I think we should still keep him on our list."

Carly laughed, "Our extremely short list."

Knowing there had to be even more to the footage Pilot eagerly pushed the rewind button. "Okay, let's replay it and see what we missed."

Immediately upon replaying their footage, Pilot ran a side-by-side comparison to the bank's security cameras. Right away, they saw the back of Bo's head enter the bank (on both screens) and head over to where Anthony was standing against the side wall.

"I forgot! Anthony told me he worked at the bank as a Junior Security Guard," Carly explained.

The gang nodded and watched as Mr. Simonson, aka Bo, handed Anthony a pile of mail. At that moment, the two films diverged. Where Pilot's cameras kept on filming from the teller's perspectives, the eye in the sky bank security footage froze. Exactly what you'd expect from a high-quality signal jammer.

"We got them!" Maddie exclaimed, and Carly jumped up happily.

"Not to rain on your parade, but I'm not so sure. We can recognize Mr. Simonson as Bo, but I doubt the police will. And if we show them our footage without hardcore proof it is the Dylans, you know they'll either kick us out before we even walk into the station—" warned Pilot.

"As they've done before," agreed Cornelious.

"Or," continued Pilot, "they'll bring us up on charges for putting private cameras in a national banking institution."

The gang was quiet and then Maddie groaned, "Since when are the boys the voice of reason?"

22

If April showers truly brought May flowers, Asbury was to have a very lush plant life following this year's April. To the gang, it seemed that they had been stuck indoors, and in their own minds, for well over a week. Ever since their stakeout and discovery of the perps, they had found themselves at a stalemate on how to proceed. They knew going to the police would be futile, but attempted to do so anyway. Unfortunately, the seemingly never-ending rain caused Asbury's finest to be even more impatient with the gang than usual. Upon walking out of the station and seeing the gang heading his way, Chief Officer Chip wheeled right around, slammed the door, and locked them out of the station. Carly, usually more even-tempered than her counterparts, ran up to the door and pounded on it exclaiming, "It can't be legal to lock up a police station!" Her friends dragged her away, and sloshed their way back to Cornelious' for sundaes and smores Pop-Tarts.

Later that week, as they sat in Study Hall, each quiet with their own thoughts, Pilot's phone buzzed with an alert.

"Mr. Owens, I believed you had more common sense than to leave your phone turned on in a library! If it was up to me, and not against school policy, our sacred library would be phone-free," lectured Ms. Cunningham. She had walked over to the group to remind Maddie that there were only two book club meetings left in the year, and seeing as she would be an upperclassmen next fall, if there were any books she would like to recommend. Inwardly sighing and outwardly politely smiling, Maddie thanked her teacher and assured her she would compile a list of winners.

Satisfied with her mission, Ms. Cunningham smiled at Maddie, but made sure to scowl at Pilot before twirling her long, gray skirt in a grand gesture—ensuring everyone knew she was still upset about cell phone usage amongst her beloved books.

Once she was out of hearing range, Cornelious whistled low and ran his hand through his hair smiling, "She really does detest anyone who's not in her club."

"That's not true," Carly replied, offended at the idea that someone would not like her.

Pilot glanced at his girlfriend quickly, but knew better than to argue. Instead, he looked at the update that had popped up onto his phone screen.

As Pilot read through the official police update, Carly continued, “Ms. Cunningham may only allow a certain type of person into her precious book club, but that doesn’t mean she hates everyone else.”

Cornelious grinned, “Oh yeah? I dare you to go borrow one of her literary classics that she keeps encased in that glass shelf behind the check-in counter when you first walk in.”

Carly rolled her eyes, “That’s an unfair dare! She never lends those books out to anyone.”

Cornelious leaned back and smiled victoriously, before putting his arm around Maddie. “Huh? Is that so? I could’ve sworn our girl Maddie here, borrowed a Joseph Heller signed ‘Catch-22’—that is currently right smack-dab in the middle of that case—just last month.

Carly’s mouth dropped open and slit her eyes. “That’s not… that’s not possible.”

Maddie shrugged, “It’s not a big deal.”

“Yes, it is! That’s bias! A book club bias—I can treat books just as well as anyone… the nerve of her to be so…so…so mean!” Carly exclaimed in a heated whisper, not daring to invite Ms. Cunningham back over to their table, this time to reprimand her.

Before Cornelious or Maddie could answer their heated pal, Pilot popped his head back up and steered the conversation away. “Guys, I just got an unofficial-official-police-update, so only we know this now, but… the Hankins’ just had a large sum of money withdrawn from their account. In fact, it was a double withdrawal, as the thieves—"

“The Dylans brothers,” Maddie interrupted.

"Yes, the Dylans, took money from both the Hankins family personal account and his business account for his psychiatrist office. Man, oh man, that's got to hurt bad…especially if the IRS chooses not to believe the money was stolen and decide to audit…"

"Pi, focus."

Pilot blushed and sat up straight. "Right. There must be a pattern that we're missing."

"I don't know. It seems pretty random to me, and we've tried to flush out every possible rhyme or reason for them choosing who they choose," Cornelious stated.

Maddie bit her lip, but agreed with Neal. "I agree with Neal guys. Crooks don't always employ patterns. Sometimes, they take what they could get."

The gang was silent, but then Carly had a slow-building thought begin to take shape. "Yes… but how? How do they 'get?'—as you just put it."

"Huh?" Pilot asked.

Carly exhaled impatiently, "How is it these two brothers are getting all the necessary information on their victims' identities?"

Maddie's eyes lit up. "Carly! You're a genius! That's the question we should have been asking all along! How is it they know all that they know?"

Before any of the four had a chance to solidify their thoughts any further, the bell rang prompting them to leave the library, but promising to meet up at Carly's immediately following school.

******

"I love coming to your house," Cornelious groaned, as he plopped down on the floor, resting his hand on his stomach. Leaning against, rather than on, Carly's gray tufted chaise lounge Cornelious often thought that this is what his sister's room would've looked like—if he had one. Even the white baseboards seemed perfectly manicured and sparkly, just as Nancy Gibbz preferred them. Along with a massive, bedroom-sized walk-closet, that featured a constantly evolving wardrobe, Carly also had a fireplace with a flatscreen mounted above it, on the wall across from her bed. Looking around, Cornelious wondered if his mother had ever gotten around to asking his friend if she could aid in her Sweet Sixteen party preparations.

Maddie laughed, and sat down cross-legged next to him, opting for the floor rather than the 'psychiatrist chair' as she referred to it. "I agree, but you have got to learn self-control. All because Mrs. Cosentino baked a whole tray of triple layer, quadruple chocolate marshmallow fudge banana brownies, doesn't mean you have to eat the whole pan."

"I didn't," Cornelious protested weakly, "You each had one or two yourself."

As the girls laughed, Pilot went over to Carly's Queen-sized bed and pulled out a computer.

"Woah, you two ARE serious." Maddie smiled and rose her eyebrows at her two lovebird friends.

Carly and Pilot blushed, and sweetly smiled at each other. Cornelious, feeling a little better, but still way too full, joined in, "Yeah. I mean, keeping a spare computer under your girlfriend's bed. You two better slow down."

Maddie and Cornelious laughed, but Pilot just warned them, "I keep technology at every house I go to regularly, whether they know it or not."

Maddie and Cornelious' laughter died down instantly. Knowing Pilot and how likely this was to be true, they were equally disturbed.

"Wait, seriously?"

"Dude, that's spying!"

It was Pilot and Carly's turn to laugh. "The truth is, you'll never know if I'm being serious or just messing with you. Because I definitely have miniature undetectable technological instruments that I have invented, for just those purposes."

"Pi, that's just creepy." Cornelious crossed him arms, and vowed to hire a private contractor to sweep his room when he got back. He'd tell his dad it was to make sure the house was secure against political enemies. He was sure Jeremiah would be proud.

"Not to mention, sneaky…" Maddie began, but then smiled. "That's it! The answer to our problems."

"I'm almost afraid to ask," murmured Carly, sitting down next to her boyfriend, and linking her arm with his.

"I propose we sneak into the Dylans' and do some snooping of our own." Maddie rose a finger high in the air in judicious proclamation.

"Another break-in?" Carly asked, not so sure she wanted to make breaking and entering a habit.

"Look at it this way, we might be able to find out for sure if Brett Dull is involved… or at least iron out just how they know so much intimate details of their victim's lives." Maddie pointed out.

Pilot immediately began evaluating the Dylans' security features, while the rest of the gang plotted out their next adventure.

23

As luck would have it, the very night that the gang decided to venture into the Dylans' household, the rain miraculously stopped. Additionally, almost everyone in Asbury was so used to the rain, that it took a while for them to realize it was a rather nice day out. That the evening promised to be a perfect cool May night, only added to the excitement. Hopefully, it would be the first of many.

When Trent arrived to pick up Mia for their date, the two were in such high spirits that they offered to drop Carly off at Split Park—where the gang had planned to meet. During the drive, Mia remarked on how many people were out and about.

Trent laughed, "You'd think they'd never been outdoors before."

Carly nodded, as she realized that the town of Asbury was reacting to fresh air and outdoors the same way a forgotten child star would when suddenly given the lead role in a highly anticipated movie. Nervous at first, but eager to get busy.

Stepping out of the car, Carly thanked her sister and Trent, then searched for her friends. Pretty much all of her classmates were taking advantage of the break in bad weather, and she recognized half of her squad were flipping around on a clear patch of grass. Her need-to-know-what's-going-on mentality almost drove her over to them for an enjoyable few snippets of gossip. However, the more responsible side of her checked her watch and knew she should be on her way to Pi, Maddie, and Cornelious. She hurried by Jazz and the Nooks, who were sprawled out on a large gold and brown carpet, writing new hits. Carly waved and gave a bright smile when she realized the freshman clerk from MEME's was sitting awfully close to Tyler. Speeding up, she saw her friends across the park, hunched together in some scheme, she was sure.

The two boys and Maddie were leaning against a tree, rehashing one more time the layout of the security system. Just like Boy Scouts, they knew how important it was to 'always be prepared.' And lucky for this gang, they had a tech-genius handy. Pilot not only mapped the Dylans' security system, but he knew how to bypass it all. And, he bragged, it only took him under four minutes. Knowing that Pilot wouldn't reveal his ways, and that they wouldn't have understood them if he had, the gang was content with his intel.

As Carly caught up to her friends, it seemed the

fresh air and good spirits were contagious. In fact, standing outside next to one another, they felt as if the weather has rejuvenated their seemingly hopeless case. And though everyone was smiling, an undercurrent of anticipation ran through the foursome.

"This is good." Maddie grinned, and beheld the packed park. "This good weather increases the chances of the Dylans being out even longer than just having dinner reservations."

Earlier that week, the group had used one of Pilot's untraceable robots to call the Dylans and alert them to the free meal they had won. Mrs. Dylans was so overjoyed that she didn't even question how her name had been entered. If she had, the gang was prepared to explain that it was an anonymous, vote-your-neighbor-in type of deal.

"True," Pilot said nervously, "although if we need someone to hang back and be our eyes to the world, I'm volunteering myself."

"And let me go in there alone?" Carly asked, feigning hurt.

Pilot stuttered, his face matching the color of his hair. He didn't mean to sound so cowardly. He reasoned that he knew the technology better than anyone, and would be able to alert them quicker from the outside. Also, truth be told, he thought he would just be a bigger liability going in, than hanging back. "No. I didn't mean it like that… plus, you won't be alone… I just thought… you know…"

His three friends laughed and revealed that they had already planned for Pilot to be hiding outside. And a good distance from the house, in case the Dylans suddenly returned and they needed warning.

"And for distraction purposes too," Maddie pointed out.

"Wait, what?" Pilot felt himself reddening again. "How am I supposed to distract two known criminals from entering their own home?"

Carly leaned over and kissed Pilot on the cheek, "You're smart, you'll think of something."

Cornelious jumped on his bike and pat his increasingly nervous friend on the shoulder, "Let's also hope it doesn't get to that point. Just tell us to leave and we're out."

Pilot swallowed a dry lump in his dry throat, and followed his friends on their bikes. After breaking into the Pancake Brothers' last summer, he thought he had overcome his fears of being caught. The only difference then was that he was adamant that something was fishy, but no one believed him. He supposed having to prove himself gave him courage. He smiled inwardly, realizing that's pretty much how he ended up finally asking Carly out.

Getting to the Dylans' house proved to be a bit more difficult than they imagined. It really did seem as if everyone was out and about, and although fortuitous in some ways, being noticed by the neighbors could prove to be their undoing. The gang hid their bikes on the side of Nya's house—she was the type to stand by her friends and never ask questions, so they felt secure in this decision—and Pilot stationed himself down the street from the Dylans', at the corner under a big oak tree. In fact, with it being so nice out, the gang banked that nobody would bother asking a well-known computer geek why he was sitting against a tree, on his computer. After a few minutes, and multiple passerbys, their hypothesis proved correct. Pilot gave them a thumbs up, as Carly, Cornelious, and Maddie began their mission. The three of them knew that if they took the sidewalk in front of the houses, their chances of success went down pretty much to zero. Hence, they turned the corner of the Dylans' block and craftily crept their way along the shrubberies and fencing connecting all the backyards/property lines in this street. The Dylans' house being the third one in, made for quick work.

"It's almost like the landscapers of this street sculpted the backyards with the intention of allowing people to creep along them unseen," Cornelious whispered.

"Yeah, I bet they're called Sneaky 'Scapers," Maddie laughed.

Carly smiled, happy to focus on something other than breaking and entering. Although she was all for this plan, she still never felt fully comfortable breaking into other people's houses. In fact, if they didn't have the bank video footage, she doubted she would've joined her friends on this escapade at all.

Cornelious continued, "Their motto could be: We shape your plants, to hide miscreants."

Standing in the shadows, Maddie tossed a rock in front of the back deck. A single security light on the back porch clicked on, letting the gang know they had reached their destination. Staying low and in as much shade as possible, the threesome crept up to the back door.

Through a walkie-talkie-like earpiece (for cell usage is easily traceable nowadays, compared to good-old fashioned walkies… in case they were caught), Pilot let Cornelious know the layout of the house, and the keycode to the back door.

"Seriously? 1234 is the code?" Cornelious muttered in disbelief. "These guys are clever enough to rob banks but can't change their passcode?"

Maddie looked at Cornelious strangely and he knew she took his words more seriously than he had. "I mean, it's probably their parent's choice… but, that is strange."

Carly knew her two friends were likely to stand there, looking at each other—practically telepathically speaking to each other—if she didn't get them moving and focused. "C'mon guys. Mull over it later."

Making a mental note to do just that, Maddie and Cornelious joined Carly as they edged their way slowly into the Dylans' household. Luckily, no one was home, and the downstairs looked pretty empty—barely any family pictures or clutter anywhere. But then again, Mr. Dylans' was in the armed forces, which meant he ran a pretty tight ship.

Because it was a ranch-style house, it was fairly easy to find Anthony and Bo's rooms. They were located at the end of the hall, to the left of where they had entered the house. The rooms faced each other and stood wide open, as if inviting anyone to search them. Besides the usual clutter and messiness of teenage boys, there wasn't much out of the ordinary. Carly found the signal jammer pretty easily, just sitting on Anthony's desk next to a huge pile of mail.

Maddie reasoned that their parents probably had no idea what a signal jammer looked like, and probably thought it was an old-school radio. Plus, the police didn't even know about the signal jammer, which further made the probability of the boys hiding it even less likely.

In Bo's room, Cornelious found a 'Best Little Brother Award,' and Carly pulled the same out of Anthony's closet too stating, "This must be homemade or store bought from their mom or something… plus, you'd think Anthony's would at least say Best BIG Brother."

Other than even more piles of loose mail strewn about the room, there was nothing else incriminating or out of the ordinary.

"Should we take a piece of mail?" Carly inquired, picking one up to inspect. She frowned at her two friends, who were busy snooping on their own. "Guys, it's not even addressed to or from them. This one is for Hailee, and is written from Amber… Weird, right?"

Maddie shrugged, and Cornelious said it was better to just leave everything as it was.

"At the very least, they could be running a mail fraud," Carly murmured.

"Guys, the Dylans' family car is pulling out of the restaurant," Pilot's voice crackled through the silent home.

"Roger that," Cornelious replied. "I've always wanted to say that," he gushed, laughing.

The girls joined him in laughter, and the three of them silently crept out of the house and back to Pilot. Reaching the corner where Pilot was waiting, they saw the Dylan's car pull up to the stop sign up the street, and felt safe in the knowledge they had been successful.

"What should we do now?" Pilot inquired, eager to hear what his friends has found.

"I think we should find Chip and tell him about all the signal jammer, and where to find it. And, if they choose not to listen, we can even anonymously leave them the bank footage we have, since, thanks to Pilot, there's no way to trace it back to us," Carly said, pulling herself onto her bike.

Maddie groaned, but knew her friend was right. She had wanted to solve the case herself, and even catch them in the act, but she knew this was the best course of action.

"I don't even think he'll bother listening to us," Cornelious warned, turning his bike in the direction of the station.

"We should at least try… it's the right thing to do, and honestly we're at a dead end," Carly told her friends, and started pedaling.

The three of them jumped on their bikes, following Carly to the station. As they quietly biked to the Asbury PD, each was lost in their own thoughts. Unbeknownst to the gang, they each had a sneaking suspicion they had missed something crucial.

Pulling up to the station, they barely had a chance to unbuckle their helmets when Chip himself appeared, escorting an exhausted-looking Mrs. Hankins outside.

"I know, Mrs. H., we'll find them. I promise. Just, once again, try not to share any personal information with anyone."

Mrs. Hankins let out a wry laugh, "It's not like I have very many secrets. Honestly, everything the thief knew weren't things that I don't talk about everyday anyway. The teller said it herself. She admitted that she conversed with the person making the withdrawal about the dress I was so excited to buy… and Mr. Hankins' new glasses—and even what I thought of them! Heck, I told half the town of Asbury those two things myself!"

The gang listened, intrigued and surprised they weren't noticed, yet.

"I understand that, but you also said you didn't tell anyone about your recent lottery winnings totaling ten grand—"

"Except my sister, and I only told her through snail mail! I don't believe in the electronic email," Mrs. Hankins interjected.

Pilot slapped his head and whispered, "*Electronic email*? That's just redundancy, of course email is electronic!"

"Ssshh!" Carly, Maddie, and Cornelious said in unison.

Pilot shook his head sadly, but remained quiet.

Mrs. Hankins pulled her brown leather purse closer to her pink jean jacket and sighed, "I'm guessing you think I should just stop trusting everyone."

Officer Chip let out a dramatic sigh, and performed a strange tiptoe-hop from one side of Mrs. Hankins to the other, all the while holding her hand and leading her to her white Lincoln. Although it was meant to look like a sympathetic gesture, to the gang—who often remarked on Chips' resemblance to a Chip and Dale dancer—the move looked choreographed and they chuckled, as they tied up their bikes to the bike rack and waited.

24

When it became clear that Officer Chip had led the shaken Mrs. Hankins to her car, only to then speed away on some other business, the gang swallowed their pride and entered the unwelcoming police headquarters. Hoping that Asbury had hired at least one new, competent cop, Maddie stepped forward and asked Maria Scott if they could speak to someone on duty.

Maria, having twice learned the importance of these four teens, sipped the last of her iced-tea, and buzzed over for any available officers. Secretly, she pulled out a writing pad and a pencil and laid it on her lap. In the very least, she'd get some good gossip.

"You didn't happen to have any new hires recently, did you?" Cornelious asked conspiratorially, leaning on the crook of his elbow across the counter.

Confused, Maria looked up at her brother's charismatic friend and shook her head no. Before she could ask why, the circus-like due of Officers Swanson and Tennett exploded through the doors.

The partners' conversation died down immediately. The two glanced at each other and half-grinned, half-frowned---if possible. They growned.

"Are they growning at us?" Maddie whispered to Cornelious, who, agreeing, laughed in reply.

"And what exactly is so funny?"

"Yeah, and what is so important that you have to interrupt our tireless police work?"

With the utmost patience and skill, the foursome refrained from exchanging looks and stared at the two clearly annoyed officers. They only had one chance for these two to take them seriously, and they were pretty sure the laughter just killed their only opportunity.

"It's about all the missing money that has been withdrawn from the bank this past year," Cornelious began, taking a step towards the two.

In harmony, the two officers groaned. Officer Swanson looked down, as Officer Tennett looked up, giving the gang the sneaking suspicion that they had practiced this dramatic reaction beforehand, and were just awaiting the chance to use it on them.

To be fair, the two Officers, who were best buds outside of work too, did, in fact practice their entrances and reactions. As they both became policemen due to their love of crime movies, they also believed that such movies were so popular because of the mannerisms and characteristics of the officers, rather than the actual plot (in this line of thinking they were alone, of course). Needless to say, the two spent many off-duty hours consumed with studying old police movies and practicing the interactions on each other.

"Here we go again… so you four think you know all about the identity theft that is running rampant. Not only in this town, but in surrounding ones as well?" inquired Officer Swanson, tapping his hands against his rather large stomach.

Sensing the teens did not know about the widespread area of the crime, Officer Tennett took it as a victory. "Exactly. You four had no idea that we're working with Mainland and Dublin on this one, did you?"

"Whether we knew about that or not, is besides the case." Maddie angrily countered. "We know who's to blame!"

"Yeah, let me guess. The mastermind is another student at Asbury High?" snorted Officer Tennett, securely holding onto his belt with both hands, while cocking his head to the side.

"Actually, yes." Cornelious confidently replied.

Both Officers snickered. "That's a laugh. Listen kids, quit while you're ahead. You were right about it being a high schooler before…" Swanson began, holding his right elbow in his left hand, as he pointed his right finger at the group of teens.

"And the treasure hunters," Pilot stepped up, angry at being overlooked once more.

Tired of the conversation, and running out of their practiced routines, Officer Tennett leaned his long frame down so that the tip of his nose was touching Pilot's. "We.

Are. Done. Here."

The two officers nodded to Maria, who buzzed them back inside, leaving the teenagers speechless, but not surprised. Before the four of them could leave, Maria eyed the door and whispered, "I hate to sound like I'm going behind anyone's back… but you kiddos are two for two and that's more than just luck in my eyes… keep up your investigations and once you have something rock solid, let me know." Pausing for a quick second while she scribbled something down, she ripped out a corner of her notepad and handed Cornelious a small piece of paper. "It's my number—for business calls only," she warned, as the foursome solemnly nodded their heads.

Feeling like they actually had an ally, the group quietly headed home. As they walked along the concrete pathway leading from the precinct (or to depending on the direction), they saw Asbury's usually cranky tech store owner, Mr. Rhodes, looking cranky. Although his ever-present shades were blocking his eyes, his whitish blonde hair was pulled back into a tight low ponytail matching his tight-set lips that sent a stern message to onlookers that he was here to do business, and do so without glee. The gang would have happily stepped aside and let him pass, as most tend to do with Mr. Rhodes, had it not been for his sobbing wife clinging both to his arm and her kerchief at the same time.

Pilot, being the only person in Asbury whom Mr. Rhodes respected and therefore was polite to, ventured up to the unhappy couple and asked if everything was okay.

"Ah, my man… I wish I could say it was… apparently we were hacked and lost a substantial sum of money." It seemed Mr. Rhodes was speaking more to his wife than to Pilot. He held up his free hand and continued, "I know what you are going to say. Didn't I know better than to put any personal info online? Well, yes *I know better—"*

Sniffling, Mrs. Rhodes abruptly cut her husband off, "As do **I**. I only ever wrote about Brett retiring and selling his share of the store to us, which made us 100% owners, to *your* grandmother—whose name is… I guess now, ***was,*** our password… And you know she has no email and is hard of hearing so all news to her is explained via good old-fashioned paper and pen! Nothing electronic!"

Pilot offered his apologies and, not wishing to get in the middle of a domestic dispute, the gang crept away towards their bikes.

When they were a good distance away from the precinct, Maddie glumly stated, "So that pretty much vindicates Mr. Dull."

"Yeah, now it makes sense why he was able to afford that necklace, and why Mrs. Dull mentioned they were selling their house and moving into Duma Condos on the East side." Carly added, remembering how her excited Computer teacher had revealed the news to Hannah and herself, just a few days prior.

Pilot, still deep in thought over the tech-store owners, raised a nagging suspicion, "It seems like all these victims sent letters to people, which ended up being used against them."

Thinking it over, Cornelious understood, "Yeah, you're right! That means they must be reading their target's mail!"

"Which is a crime in and of itself," Maddie muttered.

Carly stopped pedaling, causing the gang to stop and look back at her beaming smile. "Once again," she slowly stated, "I correctly found a clue you all missed… Bo and Anthony had piles of mail strewn all over their room."

Although proud of their friend, they all groaned, knowing they wouldn't hear the end of it for a while. At least now, maybe she wouldn't be reminding them of cat hairs every so often… hopefully.

25

After a few tedious days had passed, and there had been no arrests (publicly or privately made), Asbury awoke to begin its annual metamorphosis from a sleepy coastal ghost town, into a booming summer oasis, for both residents and shoobies alike. Granted, most stores stayed open year-round. However, it was now that the few summer-only spots commenced opening their doors and dusting off their shelves.

Local students (mostly West-siders) wanting to make money, started applying for summer jobs. Nya and Ana, hoping to repeat the success of this past year's basketball season, applied for summer jobs at Henry's Hardware, where their boss would be Ana's father. Thus, the best friends were able to schedule their work time around their workout plans. They urged Maddie to apply too, but after last summer's escapades she had a substantial savings account. Plus, she was well on her way to a full soccer scholarship. College coaches were now able to start reaching out via mail. Although NCAA rules prohibited anything official, both she and Cornelious had lists of potential colleges that were interested in them, and vice versa. Therefore, she was committed to training harder and, if needed, picking up babysitting or PETROZZA AUTO shop shifts. Perhaps even Gibbz-catering shifts, if the desire arose.

To Maddie's annoyance, the only thing seen more frequently than 'Seasonal Help Wanted' signs, was that of her red-headed arch-nemesis. The past week, Alexis had busied herself going around school reminiscing on last year's popularity as Caulfield's Candy girl—which also made her a regular headache on the nightly town news.

"Last year really was the icing on the cake," Alexis loudly proclaimed by her locker. One of the few unfortunate aspects of school for Maddie (for she really loved Asbury High), was situated directly across from Maddie's locker. Though specific hallways were designated for each class' lockers, and those lockers ran in alphabetical order, Maddie had the misfortune of finding her own locker directly across from her public enemy number one.

It was at Maddie's locker that the gang was meeting up to embark on the next leg of their investigation. As usual, Carly and Pilot were late. This left Maddie and Cornelious stuck actively attempting to ignore the exceedingly loud conversation happening behind them.

"How could it be this hard to ignore her all of the time?" Maddie muttered under her breath, while packing up her backpack.

"I thought you dealt with candy and not cake…" Hannah intoned, rather confused.

Jason laughed as he leaned back against the lockers surrounding Alexis'. "Man, you really take things literally… no wonder we're in all the same classes."

"We are?" Hannah asked, looking strangely at Jason. "I thought Pilot Owens was in all of my classes. Is it possible to have all three of us in all the same ones?"

Alexis and Jason shook their heads at each other in incredulity, and continued their conversation. "It's just, I've realized how much of a stage presence I truly have. It's my life's calling."

Cornelious looked over his shoulder to where Alexis was talking loudly for him and Maddie to hear. He wasn't surprised to see she was unabashedly looking directly at them as she talked.

"I've decided to intern at the Asbury News this summer… and my father managed to get me my own segment."

"Cool. What's it about?" Jason asked, suddenly interested that his hot girlfriend, albeit usually-annoying-hot-girlfriend, would be on TV all summer, giving him a good chance to find himself on the airwaves as well.

"I'm not 100% set on the whole concept yet… but I have time. I start at the end of June." Alexis bragged.

"Woah," Hannah said in sudden amazement. Maddie and Cornelious turned around to see what had shocked their absent-minded friend.

"I know! I'm so excited!" Alexis glowed as if she had already won an Emmy, and Jason bent over to plant a kiss on her cheek.

Hannah placed her hand on hip, lost in thought, "Not that… I mean, that's weird… how do you start at the end of something."

Cornelious and Maddie faced each other and snickered. When both Jason and Alexis gave her blank stares in response, she shut her locker and sighed, "You said you start at the end of June. That's got to be hard to figure out."

Alexis studied her friend and then, with a sigh herself, closed her locker and grabbed Jason's hand. Cornelious and Maddie were happy to watch the threesome walk away. As they disappeared from view, Carly and Pilot turned the corner hand in hand, blushing.

"What's up with you two—or is it something grossly romantic?" Cornelious questioned.

"All because your first girlfriend was Alexis doesn't mean love is gross," Pilot responded.

"WOAH! Okay, no. She was never my girlfriend. We went to that dance last year, yeah. And she texted me a lot this year—and okay she did kiss me on New Year's Eve—but I never, ever considered us dating or a couple," Cornelious spat out quicker than a peregrine falcon diving after its' prey.

"He's kidding, none of us considered her your girlfriend," Carly added, placing a calming hand on her friend's shoulder. "Right guys?"

Maddie and Pilot exchanged looks which clearly meant they did consider her his sort-of girlfriend, but decided not to disagree.

"Yeah, of course not."

"I was just messing… besides, two different teachers just told us that we were definitely the cutest couple in all of Asbury," Pilot gushed.

"Which means we could get a yearbook superlative!" Carly squealed.

"Did you just squeal?" Maddie asked.

"No." Carly crossed her arms and glared at her friends, daring them to say otherwise.

"I think you did," Cornelious laughed.

"Anyway," Pilot interjected, breaking up the possible verbal bout that was about to ensue, "it's still two years away, of course, but it was nice." He looked over at Carly and they both smiled, visibly lost in their own world.

"Back to Earth, lovebirds," Maddie snapped her fingers, and pointed to the doors. "Time to go and crack this case wide open."

"We already know whose been ripping everybody off, so it wouldn't exactly be wide open, Mads." Carly pointed out, still stinging from Maddie's jest.

"What she means is, let's go track down those creeps, find hard evidence, and turn them into Chip." Cornelious slung his bookbag over his right shoulder, leading the way outside.

The gang confidently headed outside the high school and towards the boardwalk. Most people tend to stick to a somewhat daily routine, especially teenagers. With school taking up most of the day, the few free hours they had before passing out for the night was either filled with employment of some sort, various forms of extracurriculars, schoolwork (it's not enough to do work in school apparently), video games, or just general downtime. The Dylans brothers, when not scheming to steal or literally stealing, were creatures of habit. After a long day's work of slacking off at school—neither brother cared enough to try academically, athletically, or artistically—they headed to Brady's to wolf down some grub. This became especially obvious when multiple times throughout the past school year Maddie or Carly found themselves at Brady's being hit on by either brother. And, although Anthony was employed part-time at the bank, they saw his schedule was mostly weekends, with one or two other evenings a week. The gang further knew that today he was off of work, and they were hoping to entrap them in some criminal act.

Therefore, the gang knew they had a forty-minute window in which the brothers would be kept busy at Brady's. Deciding it was best to remain unseen, the foursome huddled under the boardwalk ramp, awaiting the brother's departure from the restaurant. Maddie and Cornelious finished an Algebra packet, while Carly worked through a tough biology assignment… by asking her pals for the answers. They did take biology last year after all! Pilot wasn't one for doing homework, as his mediocre grades reflected. Instead, he busied himself building little sand castles, and devouring all of the food they had packed.

"Man, I wish we could've ordered some taco pancakes to snack on," Pilot complained after a half hour.

Carly, busy braiding Maddie's hair (something Maddie had only recently allowed her to do, because Carly had proven to be an expert hairstylist and braiding didn't impede Maddie's ability to move quickly in any given situation), sighed and explained, "We packed extra snacks for you Pi, and we can NOT be seen, remember?"

Pilot's stomach growled. He popped the last of the Gushers into his mouth, and dejectedly sat back.

Noticing his attitude was darkening, Cornelious offered Pilot the rest of his snacks: a bag of Sun Chips and his own Gushers. Cornelious realized he wasn't as hungry as he thought, while he sat watching his best friend's transformation. He thought of telling Maddie that her hair looked nice pulled back in a tight braid, but realized that might sound weird, and instead tried (uselessly) to concentrate on other matters.

Maddie noticed that Cornelious was mesmerized with Carly's braiding—as most little kids are when watching someone craftily style hair—and smiled at her friend's childishness. Before she could say something, the sound of the Dylans' conversation boomed from above.

"Yeah well, JB just texted us to meet him. Now." Bo's voice rang out, as the pair seemingly stopped walking right above the gang's hiding spot.

"I'd still rather just call him." Anthony sounded unsure, and a little afraid of the thought of coming face to face with the 'fearless' Pitbull leader. Even if Maddie, Pilot, Cornelious and Carly weren't threatened by the big, blonde bully, they were in the minority. The Pitbulls had grown in notoriety over the past year, and were to blame for many petty crimes (siphoning internet and stealing car rims among their most frequent). Unfortunately, the gang of misfits knew how to evade the law, and Asbury's finest were unable to do more than give them a 'stern talking to,' as Chief Chip liked to call his brushes with the gang.

Anthony shuffled his feet on the boardwalk above them, “Come on, bro. It’s not that big of a deal.”

With the decision to meet JB made, the brothers continued down the boardwalk ramp. Peering out from their hidden location, the foursome watched the two teenagers walk a block to their parked car. Luckily, the gang knew where to find JB and didn’t waste time following the thieves. After a swift twenty-minute bike ride, the foursome found themselves on Pitbull terrain.

Stashing their bikes half behind, half inside of, an overgrown bush, they crept forward to the unkempt apartment complex that was the current home to the Pitbulls—or the dog house, as Pilot cleverly referred to it. Even with a man standing guard in front of building number one, all Cornelious had to do was throw some poppers (shrewdly saved from the past New Year’s Eve celebration) to the right of his post. Seemingly startled out of a daydream, the guard grabbed his ‘intimidating’ wiffle-ball bat, and sprinted around the corner.

“Wiffle-ball?” Maddie asked, holding back laughter. “Who would that hurt?”

“Me.” Pilot responded, picturing himself being batted to death by JB. Although his friends never showed JB fear, Pilot wasn’t so brave. He knew how quickly and easily JB could inflict pain on him, if he was ever caught on his own. The thought alone made him shiver.

Sprinting across the grounds, to the opposite side of where the guard had run off to, Cornelious loudly whispered “Hurry up.” Wasting no time, the trio followed suite and all four teens ducked and dashed straight for the dead, yet extremely dense hydrangea bush conveniently located under an open window into the Pitbulls' 'Oval Office.'

From their concealed position, Pilot, Maddie, Cornelious and Carly easily overheard the conversation between JB and the Dylans'. Apparently, they had missed the beginning of the meeting, for it seemed as if they were already in the thick of it. Luckily, neither party was particularly loquacious, making it easy for the gang to immediately pick up the gist.

"Look, we're not asking how you came across this money," JB's sleezy voice resounded with authority, "but—"

"We earned it," Anthony countered angrily.

"Right. Just as I surely earn my time in detention."

Laughter erupted from the Pitbulls, and the foursome found themselves stifling their own chuckles.

A single clap of JB's hands silenced the gang. "Anyways, if you want us to keep stashing all of this cash for you, the price is going up. Ya see, we gotta look out for ourselves, seeing as we didn't realize how much we'd be, uh, protecting."

Maddie swore she could hear JB smirking.

"But we agreed to 3%!" Bo cried.

"And now it's five percent or take your money elsewhere… I'd recommend the bank but I got a feeling that's where this dough… originated."

Maddie and Cornelious faced each other and read the other's mind: JB was getting smarter. Perhaps being a crime boss had inflated not just his ego, but his mind as well. Either way, both teens began to consider the precautions they might need to start taking.

On the other side of the wall, a tense moment of silence stretched out while the Dylans' weighed their options. Finally, Anthony relented and agreed to the price increase.

Sensing this was the end of their business dealings for the day, the foursome managed to sneak unseen back to their bikes. Recognizing that to leave the complex, the brothers would be heading their way, they quickly dove into the bushes.

"He is NOT going to be happy about this," Bo whispered to his brother, a few moments after the four had safely disguised themselves in the thick brownery (for the once-green shrubbery was quite dead from lack of TLC).

As if on cue, Anthony's cell rang, prompting him to tell his brother, "Well, it's him. So, we'll see."

Putting the phone to his ear, the gang huddled closer and collectively held their breath, hoping to soak up every ounce of evidence they could.

"Yes… yes… yes, but… uh, huh. Yes… are you sure? I don't think… no, sorry. Of course."

The second he ended the conversation, Bo was all over his brother, basically hanging onto his arm. "Well, what did he say?"

"Clearly, I couldn't get a word in… but he seems to think this next theft should be our last."

Looking relieved, Bo let go of his iron grip and asked, "Who's the lucky victim this time?"

A slow smile crept across his older brother's face. "Next Saturday, the fifth of June, we shall be assuming the role of Carly Cosentino's beloved and trusted cousin… she'll be sorry she didn't accept that date now," Anthony added sourly.

Carly silently hmphed, and crossed her arms. Maddie shot her a warning glance, and both boys balled their fists at the audacity of the brothers.

With their spirits lifted, the two thieves high-fived and jumped into their two-door Sorento, eager to plan their last heist.

When the coast was clear, Pilot stepped forth and gallantly helped each friend out of the bushes. "I knew JB couldn't afford this place. I hate to say I told you so…"

Carly shot her boyfriend daggers, and addressed her friends, "Last year it was Cornelious' house, this year it's my family's bank account?! What are the odds?! Next year, it could be you guys!" Carly pointed to Pilot and Maddie.

For a second, Maddie's hazel eyes widened. Then she burst out in laughter.

"What?" Carly angrily asked, squinting her eyes at her friend.

"It's just… you two are beyond loaded… who would try to break into Pilot's or my house? Other than Santa… there's no chance."

"Please don't tell me you still believe in Santa?" Cornelious rose his eyebrow at his highly intellectual friend.

Maddie rose her own eyebrows in reply and stated, "As one of my favorite authors, Roald Dahl once said: *Those who don't believe in magic will never find it.*"

And with that nugget of wisdom, the gang quietly considered how they could best catch the Dylans brothers, and figure out who their accomplice was, before the Cosentinos' cash disappeared.

26

Every year, on the first Monday during the first week of June, Asbury High played host to a different drug and alcohol awareness assembly. The teachers loved it because their students were mentally over school by this point; other than finding novel ways to review for Finals, they were stuck daydreaming about summer as much as, if not more than, their students did.

Even Janitor Cutro wasn't as apt to 'accidentally' spill his yellow bin full of dirty mop water, in front of unsuspecting students. Some even claimed to hear him whistling in the halls, although Maddie bet it was more of a siren-like call meant to hypnotize and then attack innocent bystanders.

On the other hand, the students either loved or hated the assembly—depending on who was presenting. In the past, there had been a wide range of speakers highlighting the true danger/toxicity of drugs and alcohol to developing minds. From the exciting circus performers, to actual celebrities (thanks to T.J. Scott), to dreadfully boring Great Grandmothers Against Drunk Driving—yes, Mothers and Fathers and even Grandparents had all been booked earlier. Although for that special occasion, Trent Petrozza was able to make the most of it. Though only a Freshman at the time, Trent managed to get the entire football team to dress up as old men and hit on the elderly ladies. Let's just say it's a good thing Coste wasn't principal yet, or else they'd be in detention until they became old men in real life.

Given last year's fiasco where the speaker actually turned up drunk and high—prompting inappropriate questions and answers from the student body—this year's speaker would be much milder and highly vetted. Widespread rumors filled the school that Coste's own mother was the presenter, and the senior class had come prepared with questions.

However, as the students piled into the auditorium eagerly awaiting the assembly to begin, they were disappointed to see their town Chief of Police sashay onto the stage, decorated with his uniform and trusty laptop. As he stepped in rhythm up to the podium and plugged in, a deranged picture of what was clearly a drug addict popped onto the stage's projector screen, causing some surprised screams and nausea at the grotesque image.

"He's going for the shock factor," Maddie muttered to herself, actually glad that Chip had come to her for once. The gang had decided to (yet again), at least try to include the police in their plans. Only this time, by police they decided on specifically targeting the Chief, rather than tweedle-dee and tweedle-dum. Leaning to her right, she saw Carly was seated halfway down her row and whispered, "Psst… Carly! Tell Neal and Pi to hang around after the assembly!"

Stopping midway in a conversation with a classmate, Carly spun and answered, "What? Why?"

Maddie pointed to the stage, mouthing "It's our chance."

Carly nodded in understanding, and turned back to her conversation with the girl next to her.

Satisfied that this assembly would prove useful to her in at least one way, she leaned back in her seat and watched Chip's performance. He clearly missed his calling, as he absolutely shone on stage. With quick-witted humor and well-timed jokes, in addition to heart-wrenching sob stories, Chip had the students in the palm of his hands. He even instantly put down an annoying comment from none other than Asbury's most insufferable big-mouth, Ed. With about five minutes left, Jacklyn Metal, the girl sitting next to Maddie whose greatest talent is crying at the drop of the dime, left her seat to use the bathroom and wipe away her tears.

Sliding into the vacant seat, Eric Henry smiled and joked, "She's going to need to call a plumber to clean up those waterworks."

Maddie laughed. "Now that's not nice. You know Jacklyn, she…uh…"

"Is a crybaby?" Eric rose his eyebrows, leaning in a little closer to Maddie.

"Well… you said it," Maddie grinned. She didn't like being mean to the poor girl, but back in middle school

Jacklyn used to play soccer with Maddie. When it was time for uniform handouts, she cried that she didn't get the number ten because Maddie had already chosen it. Feeling bad, she let Jacklyn have her cherished number and played in number 3 instead (chosen to honor her favorite basketball player, the great Allen Iverson of the 76ers). The coaches and teachers were impressed, but the following year Cornelious persuaded Maddie to take the number ten, as she was the best in the town, if not the state already. Needless to say, Maddie got her jersey number and Jacklyn Metal stopped playing soccer. Which was honestly for the best, as her frequent crying and flopping on the field led to numerous penalty kicks on her behalf. Unfortunately, every single one of her free kicks went over the net and proved to be more of a waste of time than anything.

"Umm, Maddie," Eric turned to face her, suddenly looking deadly serious. "There's something I've been wanting to ask you—"

Maddie saw her friend's somber expression, but with the lights turning on and the unplugging of the computer, Asbury High erupted into a sea of voices. Loud, teenager voices, that had been forced to remain semi-quiet for the past hour.

Unable to hear Eric, and seeing Chip stepping off the stage, she couldn't let the opportunity pass.

"I'm sorry Eric, I can't hear you. But I gotta go!" Maddie boomed as she ran down the bleachers and toward the stage. As she landed on the carpeted floor, she felt a tug on her elbow. Glancing back, she realized it was just Cornelious.

"What did you say to Eric? It looks like he got

punched in the gut." Cornelious asked, stepping up beside her in the chaos of the auditorium.

Maddie turned to face her friend and glanced over her shoulder to see Eric Henry looking, indeed, as if he had been punched in the gut. "Me? Nothing. He was talking to me, but then we got interrupted… it doesn't matter. We NEED to catch Chip before he leaves. Come on!" Maddie grabbed Cornelious' hand, pulling him to the stage to join Pilot and Carly—who were doing their best to refrain the man.

Seeing Cornelious hand in hand with Maddie, turned Eric's 'punched-gut' expression, into more of a 'hit by a grenade' look. Alexis, seeing Eric's reaction, smiled rather evilly and stored away this valuable piece of information in her mind, as she skipped out of the auditorium.

"Finally!" Pilot exclaimed as his friends reached them. Carly and he had been doing their best to block Chip's exit from the building, and it was hard to tell who was more frustrated.

Carly turned towards her friends and smiled down at Maddie's grasp. Tracking Carly's eyes, Maddie quickly released Cornelious' hand and scowled. Ignoring her friend, she sidled up to Chip, "Officer, or uh, Chief… what an amazing presentation. I feel as if I can see the world through new eyes."

"Madeline." Chip's tone was as expressionless as a Cruella di Vila at a puppy mill.

Maddie gave her sweetest smile, "Yeah?"

"Give it a rest. Skip to the reason why you're detaining me, so I can get on my way."

"Okay, right to the main course it is. Did your Officers-in-training give you our message?" Maddie questioned, still smiling.

"Officers-in-training?" Chip wondered in befuddlement for a moment. Surely, his top-notch receptionist, Maria Scott, would have supplied him with a memo on any new recruits, if that was the case.

"She means Tweedledee and Tweedledum," Cornelious explained, as if that made the situation any clearer.

Making sure to obviously glare at both of her friends, Carly further clarified, "Officers Tennett and Swanson, sir."

Chip made a show to rub his temples and sigh deeply, all while looking up to the heavens. "Lord, give me strength… No. I did not receive any message. What's happening now?"

"Well, it has to do with the identity theft situation…" Maddie quickly revealed to Chip all they had learned through the course of their own investigation, and detailed their plan of entrapment.

To give him credit, Asbury's Police Chief listened patiently to the group of teens before him. Though they could be more of a headache than living with a group of jackhammer artists, they had an impressive record. Furthermore, he knew there had to be some truth to their story. However, as teens—or more importantly—as civilians, they had to learn their place.

"I'm sorry kids, but my hands are tied. I have to make sure I handle each case legally, as the law sees fit," holding his hands up to stop them from further voicing their argument, he continued, "and as civilians and adolescents, I must warn you against this plan. It is simply too dangerous, with a much higher risk than reward. So please, drop it. Go to the beach, go on a double-date, heck go play video games—just not crime ones—before I'm forced to either put you under house arrest or have someone tail you."

Knowing it would be useless to argue, the gang watched Chip exit the auditorium. Although, even his rhythmic exit would have given the Cabaret a run for their money.

27

Immediately following the assembly, the gang met up at Brady's. Whenever frustration or anger threatened to derail their day, they knew there was only one solution. Piling into their regular corner booth, Pilot, Carly, Cornelious, and Maddie treated themselves to taco pancakes and cookie sundaes. And to be honest, the two chefs were more than excited to see their favorite customers. During the off season (non-summertime for Asbury), Brandan and Dennis had been working tirelessly to create a hit new dish. Luckily for the four teens, the incredible chefs had just finished their latest masterpiece, and placed the brand-new Buried Treasure Burrito on their table.

Named after last summer's escapades, Brandan and Dennis crafted an out of this world dessert, filled with as much wonder as one would find in a treasure chest. After various permutations, the chefs took a white tortilla, grilled it in drizzled honey, stuffed it with sweet cream ice cream, cookie dough and chocolate chips, swirled in some crunchy peanut butter, smothered it in homemade marshmallow sauce, and finally dipped it in hot fudge. Only Cornelious managed to finish his, prompting the gang to declare it not only the best dessert they've ever tasted, but also the best dessert ever created by human hands. Assuming Brandan and Dennis were human and not culinary Gods.

When ample time had passed, allowing their stomachs to at least semi-digest the treasure trove, the foursome wasted no time and sped over to Maddie's. Racing through the kitchen and up the stairs, the teens made it to the second floor, before Mrs. Petrozza even realized anyone was home. To be fair, she was busy removing glue from Alec's favorite lucky sunglasses that he was planning on wearing to his eighth-grade graduation coming up. Although no one was caught in the act, there was a curious scent of Tabasco sauce rubbed into the glue.

Shutting the door to her room tight, she perused the room and walked over to one of the bookshelves, where a pile of notebook paper was stacked neatly. "Okay, we need to start writing." Maddie took the lead and handed a few leaves of paper to herself and Carly.

"Hey, don't we get to do anything?" Pilot complained. Now that they could feel the case really heating up, he didn't want to be left out of anything.

"No offense, but girls have better handwriting than boys." Carly declared, settling down onto the edge of the bed, pen poised to begin.

"Hey! Offense! That's sexist." Pilot argued, sitting down next to Carly in outrage.

Maddie and Cornelious grinned at each other, as their friends argued about sexism vs the truth. The two crossed the room to sit at Maddie's beloved windowsill seat. It was her favorite place to read and Cornelious' favorite place to enter her room. The latter explained why there was a towel folded nicely next to the windowsill, as Maddie didn't want her favorite seat destroyed by constant sneaker tracks.

Looking at his watch, Cornelious broke it up, "Guys, we had a half day because of the assembly. If we want to get the first letter mailed out today, we have to hurry."

"True," Maddie agreed, knowing the dire importance of the timeline in their plans.

"Okay, so I'll pretend to be my mom, writing to your mom," Carly said, nodding to Maddie.

"Yes. And don't forget to mention how excited you are to be writing real letters again, as apart of some women's club we are now in," Maddie explained, setting the scene.

"Okay, I'll start with that… what should I say next?" Carly asked the group, after scribbling a few lines on her paper.

Forgetting their small fight only moments before, Pilot chuckled, "You should say something impossible. So, when we catch them, it'll be obvious they read these exact letters… like how proud you are of Mia's driving awards!"

All four of them busted up at the thought of Mia Cosentino being commended for her driving. That would clearly be a lie. She was more likely to be arrested than awarded when it came to anything automobile-related.

"Good idea," Carly wiped away a tear from her eye (from laughing so hard), and furiously began to write.

After reading Carly's first letter, Maddie was satisfied. "Okay, how should I respond? Remember we need specific lies. That's the only way this will work."

Cornelious leaned in to look at Maddie's page and offered, "Maybe say Daniel and Shannon's allergies to hot sauce has been confirmed."

Maddie laughed as her pen found the paper. As soon as she began, the words began to flow quicker than the Mississippi River after a week of rain.

"Oh! And include how Sophia got a pet hamster named Charlemange," Pilot added, rising from the bed in excitement.

"Charlemange?" Maddie questioned, as did Carly and Cornelious.

"What? You said to be specific… and that's pretty darn specific." Pilot crossed his arms defiantly.

Maddie began writing again, "You're right, it's just… pretty out there."

"More out there than Mia winning driving awards?" Pilot shot back.

Maddie chortled, "No. You're right. This is more believable."

"Oh! Tell my mom how you were asked to prom by Bo Dylans!" Carly gushed, eager to relive the day when Bo had asked Maddie to the Prom—and she was only a sophomore!

Cornelious' head jerked up and he simultaneously

felt his pulse quicken and heart hammer against his chest. Even in jest he found he didn't like the idea of the criminal asking his best friend out.

Pilot laughed, "Now that's a specific lie." He sat back down next to Carly, chuckling at the thought of Maddie attending Prom… and as a sophomore. That would be rich!

Annoyed, Maddie paused to look at Carly's smiling face, "Carly, that won't work. You know that's not a lie."

Carly continued, unaware of Cornelious' current condition, "I know that… but it will give the letter some credibility. Plus, if Bo is reading the letter, he might not question the other… possibly unbelievable parts."

Maddie thought for a second and conceded, "Good point." She put her head down and added more to her letter.

"He honestly asked you to the Prom? Like as his date?" Cornelious questioned, trying to keep his cool. He found that it was difficult to keep his voice even and maintain eye contact with Maddie. For her sake, she didn't seem to notice anything was amiss.

Laughing, she answered, "Yeah, as date… about two months ago. I felt bad saying no, but I just didn't want to go. Especially as a sophomore, I wouldn't even have anyone to hang with."

"You do know that some girls try to go every year, just so they can brag about it… it's a thing." Carly pointed out.

Pilot scrunched up his face, "Doesn't that ruin the magic of it?"

Carly's face brightened as she leaned over to kiss her boyfriend, "And that is why I love you Pilot Monet

Owens. You are so cute and sensitive…"

Maddie and Cornelious quietly turned to face out the window. Both to give their friends privacy as well as avoid witnessing their lovey-dovey talk, as Miss D would probably call it.

"Anyway, back on planet Earth," Maddie said to Cornelious, "I'm almost done this letter. Want to go for a run after?"

"Yeah sure," Cornelious agreed. But then, still feeling the sting of not knowing that his best friend had been asked to the biggest event of the high school year asked, "How come you didn't tell me Bo asked you out?"

Surprised that Cornelious seemed to genuinely care about what seemed to Maddie such a small thing, she shrugged. "It just wasn't that big of a deal."

Not knowing that his pulse could quicken any more, but feeling it speed up nonetheless, Cornelious swiftly breathed out, "Getting asked out? Or getting asked out by Bo?"

She turned to face her best friend in thought. "Umm… both I guess."

"Oh… so have you, uh, been asked out before." Cornelious felt his internal temperature rising, and tried to hide his embarrassment. He was also secretly praying her answer would be a certain two-letter word.

Maddie sighed, and laid her pen and paper down on the sill. "Other than by your cousin, no. And Dane flirts with everyone, so I don't think that counts."

Realizing that didn't exactly make him feel any better, he pressed on. "But you told Carly."

"Yeah, well she was there when he asked me at my

locker."

"I see… and what if someone else had asked you to Prom?"

Maddie looked her friend in the eyes and was confused as to why he was making this into such a big deal. She began to wonder if he was actually jealous. No, she told herself, he's being a protective brother. You're not exactly his type. "I guess it would depend on the person. But I definitely wouldn't go with a future felon—or current for that matter. And once again, it's not a big deal, BUT if it makes you feel better then the next time someone asks me out, you'll be the first to know. Okay?" Picking up the pen and paper, Maddie continued to fine tune her letter to Mrs. Cosentino.

Not feeling any better, Cornelious mumbled, "Sure, whatever," while realizing that he didn't exactly like the idea of someone else asking Maddie out.

28

Luckily for the Asbury, any news of the identity theft, and/or mention of the stolen money withdrawals, hadn't spread beyond the town's borders. For once, it seemed as if people were listening to Chief Chip—who cautioned against making all thefts public knowledge, as the thief could easily run off scared (thus, causing their money to disappear with them)—if he hadn't already.

An idea to increase police presence in the bank was floated, but quickly shot down since the security footage and bank security officers saw no foul play, adding officers would just scare the perp off. And the police couldn't simply monitor every withdrawal. At least not without going through the slowly turning wheels of the legal system, and gaining approval from Asbury's citizens.

Besides, in this town, no one was comfortable with the idea of having the police monitor their accounts—as private vices and how much one withdrew from their own savings, were a matter most wished to keep secret. Knowing that follow-up questions would attempt to follow the money, to validate the legitimacy of their statements, most were uncomfortable having the way they spent their money become public knowledge.

To give them credit, the thieves were careful not to empty anyone's accounts, and knew how much East siders tend to withdraw (hint: a lot), so that their withdrawals didn't seem too crazy. Of course, the thieves didn't play within the town's socio-economic boundaries, and some of the theft occurred in the West-side. With no one agreeing to let the police monitor their accounts, there was little that the officers could actually do. And unfortunately, the thieves knew it.

Essentially, both sides of town had reasons to keep the crime quiet. For the confused victims, not only did their money go missing, but they also had to fend off claims that this whole crime-spree was a hoax. The reason being that some Asburyans adamantly believed there weren't any thefts, and it was just a matter of forgotten withdrawals, or overdrafting accounts.

For his part, Mayor Gibbz also worked tirelessly to keep all news of criminal happenings to a minimum. As a summer town relying heavily on outside funds, Asbury needed the shoobies to flock to their shores and keep their economy going with their hard-earned money. Even if they didn't bank at the Bank of Asbury themselves, any mention of crime could drive their patrons to other, safer shorelines.

Maddie warned Carly not to alert her parents, reasoning it could scare off the thieves and throw a wrench in their plan. So, on the Friday night before the planned heist, Carly sat across from her parents wondering if they were busy this weekend. After all, the Dylans had scheduled tomorrow as the date of their final heist, and Carly figured they wouldn't go through with their bold robbery with any chance of the Cosentinos walking into the bank on the same day. Nonchalantly, Carly asked her parents if they had any plans for the weekend. She was surprised to see her parents exchange secretive glances.

Her father shuffled around and rubbed the back of his head with his hand (one of his many nervous tells). "We actually have to go to Washington."

"A hiking trip? Are you getting some shots in?" Carly questioned good-naturedly.

Mrs. Cosentino chuckled and walked her dinner plate over to the sink. "Not Washington State honey… D.C."

Her dad stood up to join his wife, and handed her his plate. Carly also counted this act among her father's nervous behavior. Whenever her dad was anxious, he would move to get into close proximity to his wife. Mia called it his 'power in numbers maneuver.' Carly smiled as she realized Pilot also did this, but with her. "We have some, uh, classified business."

Realizing her parents weren't going to say anything more on the matter, Carly was satisfied to let the matter drop, and dive into her mom's cranberry-smothered Belgian waffles.

When she replayed the scene later that night at

Maddie's, she should've known they wouldn't have let up so easy. She found herself repeating everything her parents had told her—all three lines of information—at least a dozen times. It took her threatening to tell the Dylans brothers they were onto them, just to get Maddie to stop questioning her. Although, Maddie, Pilot and Cornelious still spent a large part of the evening hypothesizing why the government needed the Cosentinos. They agreed it must have had to do with Mr. Cosentino's photography, but could get no further.

Although Carly originally complained they were missing the party of the year at the Carter's house (a Senior on her squad), the group knew their best chance of succeeding tomorrow would be to get a good night's sleep. And though no one felt like sleeping, they knew they had to be up and ready before the bank opened tomorrow morning. Predictably, Carly and Pilot had quickly fallen asleep hand in hand, on the floor in their sleeping bags. Sitting back on the bed, Maddie and Cornelious went over their plan, looking for holes and tying up loose ends.

Cornelious leaned back against the wooden headboard, and stared up at the sticker-covered ceiling (a feat he and Maddie had worked on for years, vowing to cover every inch of ceiling in stickers back in the fifth grade). "I just wish Chip would've went along with it."

Maddie fluffed her pillow, and turned to face her friend. "Ditto. If only we had one more chance to convince him."

Before Cornelious could utter a reply, the two heard none other than Chief Chip's patrol car blaring in the very-near distance. Unbelievably, a stroke of good luck had brought Officer Chip to Maddie's neighborhood. Apparently, some kids thought it was funny to call 9-11 and hang up, so Chip decided to scare the little ones straight.

Without a word, Cornelious and Maddie smiled at each other, sprang from the bed, and shimmied down the tree outside Maddie's window. Matching each other's pace, the two sprinted down the street and easily caught up with their favorite Chief as he was leaving the house. Noticing the two teens, Chip looked up at the sky and muttered something to himself. Leaving no room for him to speak, Chip tolerantly listened as the two implored him to their scheme, yet again.

After hearing them out, he held up both hands quieting the duo immediately. "I'd be crazy to go along with your hijinks… but Tennett and Swanson don't have any better plan, so—I can't believe I'm saying this—I'm in."

Unable to control herself, Maddie hugged Chip tightly and (before he could change his mind), the two sped back to Maddie's and awoke their sleeping pals to update them on their good fortune.

While Maddie and Cornelious were unable to fall asleep for a few hours after Chip's decision to aid them was solidified, Carly managed to fall asleep almost immediately. Subconsciously, she was worried about going after criminals with no backup… but now she found that having the Police agree to help, eased her mind completely. Seeing as his girlfriend looked so peaceful sleeping next to him, and was warmly holding his hand, Pilot was also asleep within minutes of Carly nodding off.

After adding Chip into their scheme, Maddie and Cornelious felt even more confident going into tomorrow. Cornelious was thinking of how sweet it was going to feel to see Bo in handcuffs, and smiled at the thought. Voicing his thoughts, he said, "It'll be nice catching another set of crooks tomorrow."

"I'd never have thought the Dylans brothers would be crooks… they seemed… nice."

Cornelious, laying with his right arm was a bent under his pillow on the bed, turned his head to face Maddie. "Nice? I'd say creepy." Cornelious realized how badly he wanted Maddie to view Bo as a bad guy. Not wanting to question why he felt this way, he continued, "I'd say his niceness was all an act."

Maddie grabbed Cornelious' forearm with her right hand, and slapped herself in the forehead with her left hand, "Of course!"

Not bothering to remove himself from Maddie's grasp, he smiled. "Yup. There was no way—"

Cutting off her best friend, she sat up and faced him, "No. I don't doubt he's a nice kid, if not a little awkward… what I meant was, he's an actor! He's even told me multiple times that he went to theater camp each summer, and even I knew he's a part of the Asbury High drama club… he's actually pretty talented, it's a shame he used his skills for evil."

"I wouldn't say he was that talented," Cornelious argued. "We did catch him, after all."

"True. But that's because you're even more talented at catching criminals and spotted his lucky pinky ring on the screen… he was able to fool everyone else. Even the same bank tellers multiple times."

Satisfied that she had resolved a nagging itch in her mind, Maddie lowered herself back down, flipped her pillow over, and quickly fell asleep. Cornelious stared at his friend and switched off the bedside lamp. He was having a difficult time falling asleep, but felt contented with the knowledge that, good actor or not, it wouldn't matter once Bo was behind bars.

****

Early Saturday morning, the foursome split up according to plan. Pilot and Carly biked over to the Pitbulls' headquarters to wait until phase two of their plan was underway. Maddie and Cornelious hid across the street from the bank, in the lobby of the busy Hartman Hotel, watching a live feed from a small computer Pilot had provided. Pilot had assured everyone involved that this computer, although half the size of a traditional laptop, possessed the technology to break any signal jammer, and thus, was the only way to witness the Dylans brothers in action.

Chip wanted to arrest the brothers upon withdrawal of funds from the Cosentino account, but the gang had talked him into waiting until they left the bank and met up with their third mystery partner. Thinking it was best, he also agreed to wait outside the Dylans' household (inconspicuously, of course), in case they went home after the theft. Chip, not knowing about the Pitbull-Dylans relationship, believed the brothers were most likely to head home after their daring caper.

Though satisfied that the teens didn't insist on linking up with him at the Dylans', the Chief felt something was off. Sitting in his unmarked vehicle, he questioned why the four little sleuths would choose now to listen to him and sit out, in his eyes, the most exciting part of the investigation. Maybe, he would give Maria a call to iron out some doubts and lingering questions. Chip reached for his phone and dialed his favorite, faithful secretary.

Cornelious warned his friends against telling Chip that they didn't think the brothers would return home, but rather that they would go back to where they had been storing the rest of the money—with the Pitbulls. "After all," he smirked, "we can't show all of our cards to Chip. Adults always make things harder than they have to be and mess things up."

A few blocks north, across the street from the scene of the impending crime, Maddie and Cornelious sat in the corner of the Hartman Hotel. Pulling out the tiny computer, the duo didn't have to wait long for the action to begin. Within forty minutes of the bank opening, Maddie quickly identified a chubby, bearded young man, with square under-sized glasses as a well-disguised Bo Dylans.

The two held their breath as the disguised thief waddled up to the counter, and made light talk with the teller. After explaining himself away as the Cosentino's beloved and trusted cousin, the teller seemed content to proceed with the mandated security questions—newly added from Officer Chip to coincide with the letters.

The blonde teller swept her hair back from her face and began, "The first question asks, who is the best driver in our family?"

Bo smiled and leaned against the counter with a face full of pride. "That'd be young Mia of course. You know she just won a local driving award."

The teller smiled back. "Correct. And I did hear that," she whispered conspiratorially. Straightening up she continued in her business-like manner, "What is Mrs. Cosentino's favorite thing to do?"

"Seeing as my Auntie hates cooking and lacks any skills in the kitchen, I'd say probably ordering out—since she does love to eat," he chuckled.

The teller beamed. She was still tasting the delicious zucchini-stuffed-chicken Mrs. Cosentino had cooked her just last week. Although she was only informed of this plan prior to the start of her shift, she was happy to aid in catching anyone who deemed Mrs. Cosentino a bad cook. "Correct again… last question: What is her youngest daughter's middle name?"

Bo smiled, "Well that'd be little Carly—although she's not too little anymore—and her middle name is Jemens."

Holding back a grin, the teller nodded her head and told Bo he was correct again. Bo grinned and confidently handed over the pre-written withdrawal slip, with Mrs. Cosentino's real signature clearly scrawled across the bottom. With a slight nod of his own head to Anthony, standing guard across the room, Bo thanked the teller, grabbed his bundle of cash, and hobbled out of the bank.

29

After waiting all day for the brothers to leave the bank, while wolfing down an entire box of Oreos and six-pack of yoo-hoos from their backpacks, the duo across the street was growing restless in the hotel lobby. As it was the first weekend in June, the Hartman Hotel (although not as famous, nor as illustrious as the Luxurious Lady), had its hands full prepping for the upcoming summer season. Even though the hotel was on the opposite side of town from the beach, and on the West side of Asbury, their bottom dollar prices, coupled with their always happy ways (eerily so, Pilot often remarked), made them a prime destination for the budget-minded tourists. Or the more sensible shoobies.

Seven hours after an icognito Bo Dylans wobbled out of the bank, he returned to wait outside next to his brother's car. Only this time, he was dressed as himself and sporting a black backpack. Cornelious, realizing it was the end of Anthony's shift, nudged Maddie awake.

"I think Anthony's about to clock out," Cornelious pointed to the screen, which showed the older brother waving goodbye to his coworkers.

Maddie yawned and stretched. "I would say I can't believe I fell asleep sitting on this wooden bench… but, that was a long and boring day of staking out."

Cornelious smiled, "Who would've thought they'd rip off the Cosentinos so early in the day?"

"Well, at least we can follow them now." Maddie slid out of the bench, with Cornelious following behind her.

"Yeah, and if we're wrong about them going to the Pitbulls', then we have to tell Carly and Pi to scram before JB gets there."

Maddie and Cornelious watched as Anthony and Bo slid into their car and pulled out of the bank lot. Safely securing Pilot's laptop into her backpack, the two left the Hartman and grabbed their bikes—making sure to go unseen all the while. Straddling their bikes, the two began their slow pursuit. "It looks like we guessed right… we just have to wait until we get their confession on tape, before we call Chip to come meet us."

Cornelious grimaced, "He's going to be so pissed that we didn't tell him that we figured they weren't going home after the heist."

Maddie shrugged, "True, but if Chip was there too—even though he'd surely be hiding out—they'd know. And then they'd be gone with the wind... and the cash."

After following the brothers along the invisible

boundary separating East and West Asbury, neither Maddie nor Cornelious were surprised when the car turned right at the parking lot for Asbury's Roaring Rides (behind the boardwalk), and then made its way back north. Surmising the brothers would ultimately turn left into the self-proclaimed Pitbulls' Territory of untended, yet fully-occupied apartment complexes, Maddie and Cornelious continued straight. Once they found themselves underneath the boardwalk, they quickly stashed their bikes and full-out sprinted across the street and through the rusty wrought-iron fence.

"Well, that's just a tetanus shot waiting to happen," Cornelious semi-joked.

Maddie laughed, and the two scurried into the open doorway of brick building number three. The two only had a second to catch their breath before a loud car radio came roaring into the parking lot. Cornelious nodded to Maddie, and the two snuck out of the building and squatted down to inch along the dying, yet overgrown bushes that lined the front of each building.

Reaching their destination, the pair climbed in through the open window. The second Cornelious' feet hit the ground they heard a car door slam.

"Oh, good it's you guys!" A nervous Carly whispered from across the room, holding onto Pilot's arm for dear life.

"Yeah, but we don't have much time," Maddie responded.

"Well, come on then, into the closet!" Pilot pulled his girlfriend along, and the four threw themselves into the small coat closet next to the door. With enough cracks in the cheaply-made door, the gang didn't even have to leave it open a sliver, as they could see the action clearly, without tipping the hand at their hiding spot.

"Ouch, this is an incredibly small closet," Carly complained, virtually sitting on top of Pilot and Cornelious.

"What'd you'd expect? Not everyone has bedroom-sized closets," Maddie grumbled, as someone stepped on her hand, and pulled her hair simultaneously.

"Well—yeah, that's fair. We do have bedroom-sized closets," Carly conceded, and Cornelious shrugged in agreement.

"Shhh, guys they're coming," Pilot warned, "I hope everyone left their mics on. We need this recorded."

"I thought you bugged the apartment in advance?" Cornelious whispered to his techy friend.

"Better to be safe than sorry."

"Touché."

"Boys, shut up," Maddie snapped. Her timing was perfect, as the door flung open and in strode the Dylans brothers.

"He should be here any minute, quit worrying." Anthony stated. Walking across the room, he glanced at the open window, and threw himself onto the lone bean bag chair in the litter-strewn room.

"You'd think they'd make sure to shut the windows," Bo murmured, following his brother's gaze.

"Ha! You think they're worried about an electric bill? Or this place getting any dirtier?" Anthony sniggered.

"No… I know they siphon their electric and internet and what not… I'm just saying, with them having so much 'stuff'—"

"Stuff?"

"You know… our money, and other goods stashed around here… you'd think they'd safeguard this place so nothing gets stolen."

Anthony considered this, but decided it wasn't their problem. "Who would be dumb enough to steal from JB? Plus, this is their meeting place or headquarters or whatever they call it. But other townspeople live here too, so I doubt they keep all of their merchandise here. JB may be dumb, but he's smart enough not to trust anyone else with his 'stuff' as you call it."

Bo nodded along, seemingly put at ease by his big brother's confidence. Glancing out of the window again, he turned around and addressed his older brother. "Dude, he's here."

"Finally," Anthony grumbled, "Today's shift was especially long and boring. How does he look? Grateful?"

Bo spun around, face red with worry, "Actually he looks piss—"

"WHAT IS THE MEANING OF THIS?!"

The gang froze with surprise, as the familiar burly, red-bearded man burst into the room, eyes blazing the color of his thick beard.

Cornelious caught Maddie's eyes and mouthed "The mailman?" Only to see she was equally as surprised as him. Though all four now realized the true importance of the piles of mail in the boys' bedrooms. They also silently berated themselves for not wondering how the boys had gotten their hands on the letters—and without raising suspicion.

Anthony jumped up and held his outstretched hands

up in confusion. "What's the problem, bro?"

"Yeah, what gives?" Bo squirmed, clearly uneasy with the postman's ire.

If looks could kill, both boys would've been dead the second Postman Samuels erupted into the room. Stepping close to Bo, so that the two were eye to eye, Postman Samuels hissed, "I did NOT buy you two the signal jammer, supply you with all the information you'd possibly need, train you in the art of disguise, purchase the actual disguises and get Ant the bank job—essentially do all of the work—only to be screwed over in the end."

Bo took a calm step back, but Postman Samuels wasn't done. Grabbing Bo's shirt by the front collar, he spat out, "WHERE IS MY MONEY?!"

Anthony tried to mask his anger at Samuels' manhandling of his younger brother, and asked, "Okay, we clearly don't know what you're talking about. Let go of Bo, and we'll figure this out. We told you the Pitbulls have all of our money safeguarded."

Samuels released Bo and twisted to face Anthony, "Do I look stupid? I remember what you told me, and naturally I followed up to make sure I wasn't wasting my time… but I got a call this morning from JB—head Dog himself apparently—that you two had withdrawn the money and our business had officially ended."

The brothers looked at each other in confusion. Of course, they had no idea that Maddie and Cornelious had met up with JB earlier this week and informed him that he was about to lose his investment. Unsurprisingly, he denied knowing what they were talking about and was ready to invite them to go swimming in the ocean with him and his gang—when Cornelious offered up a different business proposition. As a 'businessman' JB's interest was piqued and he listened as the two unveiled their plan to catch the conniving brothers in action, as well as their hope to involve Officer Chip. At the mention of police involvement, JB grew cold. His temperament thawed out though, when Maddie informed JB that he would face no repercussion, for if they did indeed remove the money from him now, there was no way to trace it back to him. Sure, the Dylans could say JB was holding it for them, but how could they actually prove it?

So, with JB on board, the gang arranged for him to call the third-party mystery partner (a number only JB was given with no name attached), on Saturday afternoon, after confirmation of the identity theft. Therefore, the gang knew that when Samuels arrived enraged that JB had lived up to his side of the bargain. Additionally, while the culprits were all here, JB had his best men smuggle the stolen cash into the Dylans brothers' bedrooms through the backyard—all while Chip was staking out the front of the house.

Thus, while Bo and Anthony had no clue what Postman Samuels was talking about, the gang was smiling away in the closet, happy that everything was going according to plan.

Samuels let out a deep breath and held his hand out to Bo. "Okay, we'll figure this all out, after we look over our spoils from today."

Bo look confused, "Spoils?"

Anthony tugged the backpack off of Bo's shoulders, and tossed it to the postman.

Unzipping the bag, Postman Samuels reached his

hands inside and pulled out a stack of cash. His face took on a curious expression as he removed out a single bill, and held it up to the light. Staring inquisitively at the boys he questioned, "You got these exact bills from the bank?"

"Yup, as usual," Bo spoke up, proud of his work.

Dropping the bag at the brothers' feet, he tiredly stated, "It seems you were swindled then… these are clearly counterfeit."

As Anthony and Bo checked over the cash, Postman Samuels collapsed onto the bean bag. Placing his own head in his hands, he complained to no one in particular, "I thought that I would gain so much when I discovered I had two younger brothers… I had no idea I would lose everything."

"LOSE? You wouldn't have been able to accomplish anything without us," Anthony countered.

"Accomplish?!" Samuels laughed haughtily, "Where's the money?!"

As the fight outside the closet continued to escalate, Carly perked up, "Younger brothers! They're both younger than Samuels… Now the two younger brother awards make sense!"

In her excitement, Carly turned to see her friends' reactions, and forgot herself. By twisting around, she pushed on both Pilot and Cornelious, causing all four to push against the door and tumble out into the room.

In a jumbled-up pile in front of the now-open closet, Pilot, Carly, Maddie, and Cornelious looked up at the three stunned brothers and quickly took advantage of their shocking entrance. Maddie shoved Carly to the window and told her to run.

Carly, being the most acrobatic of the bunch, easily sprung from the window and tumbled to freedom. Unfortunately, her three friends were quickly tackled to the floor upon her departure. Carly knew their best bet was Officer Chip—who was currently camped out in the neighborhood across from her very own gated community. As a lifelong resident, Carly had biked from the Roaring Rides to her house before, but she had never ran. Not underestimating the seriousness of the situation, she pumped her legs faster and prayed Chip was still staking out the Dylans'.

Meanwhile, her friends were doing their best to stall for time, and make sure the brothers didn't decide to move them to a different location. They had no way of communicating with Carly or Chip, if the brothers took them somewhere else.

Luckily, two of the thieves were high school boys, one of which apparently still had a glimmer of hope in his aching heart.

As the largest of his friends, Cornelious was currently being held face down on the floor, with Anthony sitting smugly on his back. He couldn't see Pilot, but knew Samuels was restraining him somewhere to the left of his vision. What Cornelious could clearly see was how excited Bo looked to have his arms wrapped around Maddie, holding her close to his chest, with her arms pinned behind her back.

"I finally understand why you kept turning me down all year," Bo hungrily brought his face up against Maddie's face, speaking directly into her right ear. "You suspected me the whole time! I knew you were smart but…" he paused, turning Maddie around, so he could look in the eyes, "you know, we do have a lot of money now—"

"Bo, you idiot. Don't admit to anything," Anthony growled, readjusting his position on top of Cornelious.

"Like we didn't hear everything you guys said in the clos—umpf" Cornelious started to say, but was promptly cut off with a knee to the back.

Bo glared at his brothers, but continued to try his best with Maddie, "I was just saying, I could give you anything you want. I'm far richer than you could believe."

Postman Samuels stepped forward, still gripping Pilot tightly, "I thought you didn't know where the money was."

Apparently having his crush this close in proximity gave Bo confidence. He defiantly answered his oldest brother, "I still don't know what you're talking about… and I don't know if I actually believe JB called you to say all the money is gone. In fact, you coming here could just be a ruse to make off with the money and leave me and Ant high and dry!"

The thought of Samuels taking the money for himself hadn't occurred to Anthony until now, and Cornelious could feel Anthony squirming top of him, as if considering the validity of this new idea.

Postman Samuels slapped his forehead in frustration. "Do you think I'd risk exposure and come to this… this… this dump? Just to double-cross my own kin?"

Anthony and Bo glanced at each other from across the small room.

"What we need to do is figure out where the money is, and what to do with these three," Anthony declared, momentarily breaking the tension.

"Yes. One thing at a time," Samuels decided.

As Samuels and Anthony launched into a conversation about where to stash the three teenagers while they went to find JB, Bo tried once more to smooth talk Maddie.

"Sorry about all of this… we just have to be safe," Bo smiled. "But, I'm serious about us."

"Us?" Maddie questioned, thinking this kid must be crazy.

Mistaking her 'us' for something promising, he explained, "Yeah. I mean, now that you know the truth, we can't exactly let you guys free to squeal on us… but the bright side is we can give us a try. You know go out," Bo said hopefully.

Cornelious felt his insides tighten up, was this creep trying to ask Maddie out via kidnapping?

Apparently, Maddie felt the same way, as she looked up incredulously at Bo and voiced Cornelious' thoughts, "So you're asking me out, by kidnapping me?"

"Well… no. I mean, when you put it like that…" Bo sighed heavily. "It's just now that I know that you didn't go out with me this year because you suspected me—which you were right about—well, now nothing is standing between us."

Maddie looked deep into her captor's eyes, and laughed. "That's a mouthful." Then, without giving him a chance to reply, or even to run away from his embarrassment, "And that's not why I didn't go out with you, Bo. I just didn't, and still don't, want to."

Knowing she just pissed off one of their captors,

Pilot groaned, Cornelious smiled, and Maddie continued to laugh. That is until Bo slapped her across the face. Clearly startled from the pain and the sudden violence, Maddie stumbled back, almost tripping over the bean bag chair.

Saving her from falling over by roughly twisting her arms behind her back and shoving her to the ground, Bo spat, “Not so funny now, huh?” Luckily, Bo’s shove pushed her to her knees first, before lowering down onto her stomach, or else she would have likely broken her nose. Maddie turned and realized she was now side to side with Cornelious, who was still being held down by Anthony—although he was obviously exerting more effort now, as Cornelious was trying to push Anthony off of him so he could get up and wring Bo’s neck.

Despite the bright red hand mark on her cheek, Maddie smirked as she lay next to Cornelious.

“You always have to piss them off more, huh?” Cornelious stared daggers at Bo, after giving up trying to break free.

“He’s a creep,” Maddie muttered, working her jaw to ease her cheek pain. “But he hits like a girl—which is not a good thing, cuz girls hit HARD.”

Before either Maddie or Cornelious could communicate any further, the three brothers shoved Pilot to the floor to join his friends.

“Now, all we need is rope,” Samuels concluded, sneering down at the three teenagers.

30

Pilot whispered to his two friends, "How long do you think it will take Carly to get help?"

Not wanting to dampen anyone's spirit's Maddie didn't reply, not trusting her friend's cardio to be strong enough to get to Chip quickly enough. Ever the optimist, Cornelious whispered back, "She'll be back soon, I know it. We just can't let them take us somewhere else."

"Hey!" Postman Samuels kicked a heavy boot at Cornelious left side, instantly bruising his ribs and taking the air out of him. "No conspiring behind our backs kiddos!"

Anthony and Bo laughed with their older brother, as the thieves continued their conversation.

"Okay, this place may be a dump," Anthony stated,

motioning to the newspaper, glass, and general debris strewn across the old wooden floor. “But I don’t see any rope.”

“Or anything useful at all,” Bo added in frustration.

Samuels pulled on his thick beard, and kicked some trash out of his path. Muttering to himself, he considered how to remove three teenagers from this building without causing any alarm. “This is going to be tricky.”

“Yeah, you’re telling me. I can only sit on them for so long,” Anthony complained. Although he was only sitting on Cornelious and Maddie, correctly betting Pilot wouldn’t dare move.

“Here’s what we need to do,” Samuels began. Pointing to Bo, “Go grab some rope and duct tape. We don’t know where that blonde girly ran off to, or how soon she’ll be back. So, we need to move these three out of here ASAP.”

Studying their three hostages, Samuels explained his idea. “That one, the Gibbz boy, looks to be the strongest and there would definitely be a solid manhunt out for his safe return. Given Jeremiah Gibbz’ resources, I don’t think it’d be smart to bring him with us.”

“I agree, but I’m not killing anyone,” Anthony replied.

At the mention of murder, all three teenagers grew cold.

Postman Samuels laughed, “I may be a crook, but I’m no idiot! Of course, we’re not going to kill any of them. But we need to get far enough away, without raising any red flags. I think we leave the rich kid, and take these two with us.”

"Where?" The Dylans brothers said in unison.

"Like I just said, I'm no idiot. I'm not going to say anything else in front of the Gibbz boy." Postman Samuels got down on one knee and jerked Cornelious' head up, so that they were eye to eye. "I have a feeling you don't want any harm to come to little missy and nerd junior here—"

"Nerd Jr? Really? That's my nickname?" Pilot complained.

"That's your issue? That he called you nerd junior and not that we're about to be kidnapped?" Maddie shook her head in disbelief.

"I'd call you ginger boy, but I'm the head Ginger around here," laughed Samuels.

"Why not just call me sonny, if you called her missy?"

Losing his patience Samuels rubbed his temples and turned back to face Cornelious. "Back to my original point. What if I told you, this could be easy for everyone… we're taking your two friends and will return them to you in one week—no harm done—if you don't make too much of a fuss. However, if we so much as hear people are searching for us, then we might not be so willing to return them in one piece."

Cornelious stared back into the mailman's eyes, "Let me get this straight. You're saying you'll take both of my friends hostage, bring them to some unknown location, and if I just let you go and don't involve any authorities or whatever, then you'll send them both back in one piece."

Samuels smiled broadly, "Exactly."

Cornelious squinted his eyes in faux confusion. "So, you'll send my two friends back in one piece, or am I only getting one friend back… or are you combining them into one piece… or—"

"ENOUGH! I've had it up to here with teenagers thinking they're so clever!" Samuels boomed, as he sprung up to his feet. Grabbing Pilot roughly by the ear, the postman jerked him to his feet and motioned for his younger brothers to do the same with Maddie and Cornelious.

"We're running out of time. Let's just stash all three in the back of my mail truck, and hit the road," Samuels decided for the group.

"It seems you mailmen are quite determined. I mean, you take that motto of yours so seriously, I guess it rubs off on everything else, huh?" All six heads jerked toward the open apartment door, as the fearless leader of the Pitbulls smirked, standing tall and proud, surrounded by a handful of faithful lackies.

"Listen, we DO need to talk. BUT one of them got away and will be back any moment… so scram, kid." Samuels glared.

It was turn for Maddie, Cornelious, and Pilot to smirk. They knew the only thing JB hated more than being told what to do, was being called a kid. In fact, on his first day preschool, after each parent left their little one behind for the first time, JB poured his oatmeal all over the sweet teacher who welcomed each student with a hug and some variation of 'Aren't you a big kid now?'

JB straightened up, crossed his arms across his broad chest, but made no move to unblock the doorway. "You see, I thought I gave you a curtesy call when I said we no longer have any business. Yet, here you are, on MY turf, kidnapping… well, not my friends… but still, my classmates. How do you think that makes me feel?"

"You've got to be kidding me," Samuels growled. "This is why I knew it would be a mistake dealing with teenagers."

JB clicked his tongue and shook his head (clearly mimicking villain behavior from superhero movies), "I'd say your issue was underestimating teenagers."

Samuels tightened his grip around Pilot's wrists, and warned JB, "If you don't let us through this door, we will have to force our way out."

"I'm pretty sure they outnumber you… ow!" Pilot yelled, as Samuels yanked his wrists even harder.

"And even if you did somehow overpower us, I have a strange fifth sense—"

"Sixth sense," Maddie corrected.

"You're seriously correcting him? Now?" Cornelious stared at her in disbelief.

"Well, he should know we have five sen—"

"MADELINE! Jeeze! Give a guy a break!" JB exclaimed. Turning back to the thieves, and cracking his knuckles in intimidation, JB regained his composure and continued, "Anyway, I had a sixth sense something was wrong in my territory, and I decided to phone a friend with more say around here than all of us." JB smiled, and stepped to the side, just as Officer Chip waltzed into the room.

Similar to a needle striking a balloon, all of the air went out of the room, as Maddie, Pilot, and Cornelious each felt their captor deflate.

Chip held up his open palms, "You know, once

again you four were so persistent that you dragged my secretary into your ramblings about the Dylans brothers." Chip breathed out deeply, as Carly proudly walked into the room. "Therefore, Maria's research coupled with our meeting last night, left me with no choice but to actually take your little investigation seriously. Then after waiting outside the Dylans household, I still felt like I was missing something…so, I dug around and found Postman Samuels is the older brother to these two adopted boys." Chip fluidly motioned to the Dylans, who reluctantly released their hold on their captives. "And although Samuels is his true last name, I discovered that in Arizona he went by Postman Woltwise. Woltwise was a part of their courier service for two years before ultimately being suspected of identity theft and fleeing. Unfortunately for us, he decided to contact his only known kin and pull them into his schemes."

Pausing for dramatic effect, Chip strut over to Samuels and laid a hand on the big man's shoulders, "You know, the three of you ended up being lucky, believe it or not. Arizona PD sent information on Samuels here to Mainland PD—back in October—when they were having identity theft issues. Turns out, our communication isn't as strong as I hoped… probably because I beat out their chief in the high school play all those years ago…" Chip muttered to himself, temporarily caught in the past.

Maddie, Pilot, Cornelious, and Carly grinned at each other over Chip's admission, and felt validated that he had, in fact, been a participant in the world of dramatics (as they rightfully assumed).

Breaking out of his reverie, Chip watched the

brothers exchange glances and look to the window. The Chief cautioned, "Go ahead and try. But I wouldn't attempt any funny business. I have two squad cars parked outside waiting to escort you three to the precinct."

Samuels snorted, "You don't have any hard proof, other than the words of some teenagers. No court on Earth would convict."

Picking up the book bag from the floor, Chip turned to his favorite teens. "I wasn't so sure that using counterfeit money made by my own department would actually work. In fact, I thought the thief would notice right away, and run scared."

Maddie beamed, happy for the back-handed compliment.

"And other than wiring this room to also tape-record any conversations that happened here today, thanks to Mr. Owens," Chip nodded to Pilot, who blushed and said it was no big deal. Chip smiled and continued his speech, "but the absolute icing on the cake, was getting Bo on tape answering all of the security questions correctly… questions that we planted, I should add."

"Wait, what?" Bo asked, in confusion.

Carly smirked and crossed her arms, "You told the teller my middle name was Jemens." Not giving him a chance for denial, she continued in her best French accent, "Jemens, is French for I'm lying."

The gang couldn't help but laugh, as the brothers realized the futility in arguing, as well as any hope of escaping.

Samuels released Pilot, and held up both hands. "I want a lawyer."

Chip bowed, as if a curtain call was underway, and ushered the three thieves outside, reading them their Miranda Rights as he went.

Once Chip had removed the brothers from the apartment, Pilot ran across the room to Carly and hugged his girlfriend tightly. "I knew you'd make it to Chip in time."

Carly blushed, but looked to JB. "Actually, I didn't. I may be in killer shape for cheerleading, but my cardio isn't so perfect."

JB laughed, "That's an understatement, princess. I found you huffing and puffing near Split Park."

Carly rolled her eyes, "Yeah, well, I admit it wasn't my finest hour."

Pilot pecked Carly on the cheek, "It doesn't matter. You brought the cavalry, and saved the day!"

Carly sighed, "Like I started to say… not exactly. JB and his dogs saw me and since they knew a little about our plans, JB figured we needed help."

Maddie, Pilot, and Cornelious looked at the big, blonde bully in surprise.

JB thrust his hands in his jean pockets. "Woah. Don't be getting any ideas. I only helped because I owed Ms. Perfect here a favor. From detention… when you had my back."

Maddie smiled, and walked over to JB, extending her hand. "I'd say we're even now."

JB ignored her hand, and chose to spit next to her foot instead. Cornelious angrily stepped up to JB, but Maddie outstretched her right arm, blocking him from escalating things.

"You let your girlfriend do everything for you, huh?" JB chuckled, and turned to leave the room. "Like I said, the debt is done… don't think this means we're on the same side."

Maddie grinned, "Never."

His back to the room, JB snapped his fingers over his head and his Pitbulls piled out in front of him. "Good, 'cuz it's a long summer ahead."

The foursome waited for JB and his dogs to exit the building, before following suite.

"He's right, there's a long, beautiful summer ahead of us." Carly beamed, picturing the surf, sun, and work-free schedule in her near-future.

"Let's just hope it's a mystery-free one… or at least if there's treasure again, Asbury PD won't confiscate it," Pilot added.

Cornelious looked over his friends and laughed, "What are the odds this summer will be drama-free?"

As the gang left the apartment complex, they watched the Police lights fade in the distance to the East, as the Pitbulls gathered in a weird huddle to the West.

"I don't think Asbury is ever drama-free," Maddie intoned.

Cornelious beamed, "Then this summer will be one to remember."

NOTE TO READER:

Thank you for reading. If you've enjoyed Asbury High and the MisTaken Identities, please leave a review!

As an independent author, the best way to gain exposure and to keep more books coming, is for our fans to leave reviews. Of course, word of mouth and social media exposure is appreciated as well---but I'd love to read your thoughts on the book. So please leave a review **on Amazon and Goodreads.**

For upcoming books, more news and even to contact me directly, please visit my website at:
www.kbchannick.com

or follow me on Instagram or Bookbub at:
www.instagram.com/kellybradychannick
www.bookbub.com/kellybradychannick

COMING SOON:

ASBURY HIGH
AND THE KIDNAPPER'S DRIVE

BOOK FOUR IN THE ASBURY HIGH SERIES

ABOUT THE AUTHOR

For as long as she could remember, Kelly Brady Channick loved making up stories, and leaving her listeners/readers on the edge of their seats.

Perhaps that's why she always managed to talk herself out of trouble...

After graduating from Ocean City High School, NJ, Kelly accepted a basketball scholarship to Holy Family University, in Philadelphia. As a lifelong athlete, Kelly understands the importance of teamwork and overcoming adversity, both of which she hopes translates into her books.

Before writing page-turners, she taught first, fifth, sixth, seventh and eighth grade — like a dessert menu, she simply had to test them all out. But her favorite job is the one she's now doing full time: writing. Kelly loves to craft whodunit mysteries, leading readers through various twists and turns, filled with red-herrings, hidden clues, and more peculiar characters than you'd find in a circus.

Kelly lives in South Jersey with her handsome husband, energetic baby boy, two cookie-stealing dogs, and an awfully smart cat.

If you want to know when Kelly's next book will come out, please visit her website at http://www.kbchannick.com.

Made in the USA
Middletown, DE
24 September 2020